INHERITING A SCOTTISH CASTLE

INHERITANCE OF THE HEART
BOOK TWO

SYLVIA MCDANIEL

Inheritance of the Heart

Inheriting an Irish Groom
Inheriting a Scottish Castle
Inheriting an Alaskan Gold Mine
Inheriting an Italian Vineyard

She inherited the castle. He came to claim it. Only one will win…unless love takes it all.

When her estranged father, legendary rock star Keir MacLaren, dies, Isla MacLaren inherits a magnificent Scottish castle—and the life she never asked for. Along with it comes Keir's unfinished business, buried secrets, and one complication Isla can't ignore.

Callum Fraser.

Gritty, maddeningly capable, and infuriatingly hard to dismiss, Callum is the man Keir took in and raised after Callum's father died. To Callum, the castle isn't a prize. It's home. Proof of the only family he ever trusted. And he's not about to watch a stranger, Keir's daughter, walk in and take it from him.

Forced under the same roof while the estate's future is decided, Isla and Callum clash over everything…until heat turns to something far more dangerous. Because the real risk isn't losing the castle. It's losing their hearts.

CHAPTER 1

The last note didn't end so much as refuse to die.

It hovers above the Steinway like a held breath, vibrating faintly in the ribs of the instrument and in the lacquered wood of the stage. Isla MacLaren keeps her hands suspended over the keys, wrists lifted, fingers curved, holding the silence as if it is one more bar of music she alone controls.

The Hilton Head International Piano Competition is famous for its purity. No theatrics. No grand gestures. The music does the talking, and the pianist is expected to disappear into it.

Isla has mastered that. She can vanish right in front of a thousand people. The music hides her pain and soothes her soul. It has from the time she was a small child.

She counts three slow breaths, one for control, one for poise, one for the discipline drilled into her bones since childhood, then lowers her hands to her lap.

The hall remains silent for a heartbeat longer.

Then applause crashes over her.

It comes in waves: first the polite, immediate clapping of people trained to applaud at the right moment, then the swell that signals something else, approval turning into excitement,

excitement turning into reverence. In the front row, someone rises. Then another. Then entire rows stand as if pulled upward by the same invisible string.

The lights are hot and blinding, turning the audience into a soft blur of faces and dark clothing. Isla stands smoothly, as though her legs didn't tremble beneath her gown. She didn't look frantic, didn't look relieved.

She bows once, deep, measured.

Twice, gratitude without desperation.

She feels it in the room, the same way she feels tempo: she has them.

And more importantly, she has *herself*.

For a moment, there is only the sound of clapping and the faint scent of varnish and old velvet. The air tastes dry, conditioned, charged with the way people hold their breath when they believe they are witnessing something important.

First place.

The thought didn't come with giddy celebration. It arrives with a quiet certainty, settling into her chest like a key sliding into a lock.

She had known even before the final movement, even before she took the risk of that barely-there pianissimo in the development section. Her fingers had been calm. Her mind had been silent. She hadn't fought the piece. She hadn't wrestled it. She had simply stepped into it like stepping into cold water and letting it close over her.

Flawless.

As she straightens from her second bow, something shifts.

Not onstage.

In the audience.

A ripple moves through the hall, subtle but unmistakable. Heads turn in quick, sharp motions. Whispers spread in a low wave, not the reverent murmurs of connoisseurs but the urgent hiss of news traveling faster than manners.

Isla's gaze sweeps the crowd automatically, trained to track disruption. At Hilton Head, even a cough during a slow passage could earn you glares. Yet now the disturbance isn't a single person; it is everywhere, spreading like ink.

Phones are out.

That is wrong. Recording is forbidden during performances, and the audience here usually obeys rules like commandments. But screens glow anyway, hastily tilted down, fingers tapping, thumbs scrolling.

Her stomach tightens.

She searches for one face.

Alisa MacLaren, her mother, stands near the aisle, posture rigid, hands clenched together in front of her. She isn't applauding. She isn't smiling. The composed pride she usually wears, her controlled version of motherhood, is gone.

Her face is pale as paper.

When their eyes meet, something flickers in Alisa's expression that has no place in a concert hall.

Fear.

Isla bows one final time, turns, and walks offstage with the same poise she'd practiced since childhood. The curtain falls behind her, muffling the roar of applause. Backstage is dimmer, cooler, smelling of nervous sweat and the faint metallic tang of stage lights.

"Brilliant," a volunteer murmurs as Isla passes, eyes shining.

"Thank you," Isla says automatically, voice smooth as a practiced scale.

She keeps moving toward the greenroom, her mind already beginning the mental catalog she always does after a performance, tempo held, pedaling clean, voicing balanced, when Alisa appears in front of her like a barrier.

Her mother grabs her arm.

Hard.

"Isla," Alisa says, voice low and urgent. "We need to leave. Now."

The pressure of Alisa's fingers bites through the fabric of Isla's sleeve. Isla blinks once, startled less by the grip than by the look in Alisa's eyes, wide, frantic, unmoored.

"The judges haven't announced the winner yet," Isla says, steadying her voice. "I'm still in the final."

Alisa shakes her head sharply. "It doesn't matter."

"Of course, it matters." Isla eases her arm free, careful not to make a scene even here. "This is the final round, Mother."

Alisa's breath comes out unevenly. She glances down the corridor, toward the stage door, toward the bustling staff, then back to Isla as if she doesn't know where to place her fear.

Something cold slides into Isla's gut.

"What happened?" Isla asks.

Alisa opens her mouth. Closes it. Then places both hands on Isla's shoulders, as if bracing her against a blow.

"Your father is dead."

The words don't explode.

They arrive oddly flat, like a statement from a news anchor.

Isla waits for grief. For shock. For the sudden collapse of a daughter's world.

Nothing happens.

No image flashes in her mind. No warm memory rises. No ache unfurls.

Instead, her mind supplies the only facts it has ever been given about Keir MacLaren: famous, brilliant, absent.

Dead.

After all these years.

Alisa's fingers tighten on her shoulders. "We have to go," she says. "Immediately."

"No," Isla replies.

The word comes out calm and certain, surprising even her.

Alisa's brows knit. "Isla—"

"I just played my final program." Isla's voice stays steady as she speaks, as if she is discussing the weather. "I'm in first place."

"This is bigger than a competition," Alisa snaps.

A short laugh escapes Isla before she can stop it, sharp, almost humorless. "Is it?"

Alisa's jaw sets. "Don't do this."

"Do what?" Isla asks, and she feels the blade of anger sharpening inside her. "Pretend I'm devastated? Pretend he was a father?"

Alisa's eyes flash. "He *was* your father."

The word scrapes, ugly with expectation.

Father.

Heat blooms behind her ribs. Not grief, never grief, but something old and jagged.

"He was a sperm donor," Isla says evenly. "Nothing more."

Alisa's face tightens. "You don't mean that."

"I do." Isla holds her ground. "He didn't raise me. He didn't call. He didn't write. He didn't come to recitals or competitions. He didn't come to Juilliard. He didn't show up once, not even when I won my first international at sixteen."

Alisa flinches, and for a second, Isla sees it: not just panic, but something else, something like dread.

"He sent money," Alisa hisses, as if that should end the argument. "Every month. Without fail."

Isla saw the checks without meaning to, numbers on paper, large enough that her childhood had been cushioned, protected, polished. Lessons, masterclasses, travel, the best teachers money could buy. Alisa never let Isla forget what those things cost.

Isla has never been foolish. She understands wealth was a tool.

But it isn't love. It isn't a father's hug or his approval when she won her first competition.

"Money isn't parenting," Isla says. "Money is money."

"It paid for *everything*," Alisa shoots back. "It paid for your teachers. Your competitions. Your instrument. Your apartment. Your—"

"My life?" Isla cuts in, and the words come out sharper than she intends. "Is that what you want to say? That he bought the right to be called my father because he mailed checks from somewhere he didn't want to come back from?"

Alisa's nostrils flare. Her eyes shine with something too close to tears, but Alisa doesn't cry. Her mother has never allowed herself that kind of softness.

"This isn't about your pride," Alisa says. "This is about what happens next."

"What happens next," Isla repeats, and something in her mother's tone makes the hair rise along Isla's arms.

Alisa's gaze flicks again toward the corridor, the stage door, the staff moving past. "They're going to come for you," she says tightly. "The press. Everyone. If they know you're here—"

"Why would they know?" Isla demands, then remembers the phones in the audience, the glowing screens, the murmurs. "They already know something."

Alisa's mouth flattens. "Exactly."

A door opens down the corridor. A stagehand peeks his head out, polite but harried. "Ms. MacLaren? We'll be ready to announce shortly."

"We'll be there," Isla says without hesitation.

The door closes.

Alisa stares at her daughter as if she doesn't recognize her. As if the obedient, polished girl she had shaped into a weapon of excellence had just stepped out of her mother's grasp.

"You don't get to decide how we handle this," Alisa says quietly, dangerously.

Isla lifts her chin. "I decide how *I* handle it."

Alisa's lips part, ready to argue, then close again. Her shoulders sag a fraction, a tiny concession that tells Isla she'd won this round.

"Fine," Alisa says. "Stay. Smile. Accept your medal. But when this turns ugly, don't look at me like I didn't try to save you."

Isla doesn't answer.

Because the truth is, Isla doesn't want saving.

She wants control.

The minutes before the announcement stretch. Isla stands in the wing, listening to the murmur of the audience returning to their seats, to the shuffling of programs, the clearing of throats. She watches a pianist from another country pace with clenched hands, watches a judge speak quietly to a staff member.

Alisa stays beside Isla like a taut wire, eyes darting toward the hall, toward any door that might open.

Isla keeps her face composed.

Inside, she feels... nothing about Keir. Not sadness. Not shock. Not even anger in the way people expect anger to be, hot and emotional and messy.

Her anger is clean.

It has been clean for years.

A choice made over and over: she didn't matter to him, so he didn't get to matter to her.

When Isla was a child, she had made excuses. She had believed the stories people told about famous men: busy, brilliant, trapped by the demands of their gifts. She had imagined Keir was coming, that he would walk through the door one day with arms wide and regret shining in his eyes.

By twelve, she knew better.

By fifteen, she had stopped asking.

By nineteen, she had learned that the absence itself could be a kind of presence, a shadow that followed you into every room, shaping you without ever touching you.

Isla had decided she would not be shaped by him.

She would be shaped by practice. By discipline. By precision. By Alisa's relentless expectation.

That was the only inheritance that mattered.

The stage manager motions, and Isla walks out beneath the lights again.

The applause is polite now, the audience settling into the ceremony. The judges speak, praising artistry, technique, and interpretation. Isla listens with the same calm she wears for everything that matters. She waits for her name.

When the head judge smiles and announces that Isla MacLaren is the winner, the hall erupts again, this time with certainty, as if everyone had been holding the same conclusion in their mouths.

Isla accepts the medal. Shakes hands. Smiles in the correct places.

She does not think about Keir.

The rest of the night comes in fragments.

A photographer asks her to tilt her chin. A journalist tries to corner her for a quote. Isla declines interviews with a graciousness that leaves no opening for argument. She moves from one congratulation to the next like a dancer stepping through rehearsed marks.

Alisa hovers close, answering where Isla refuses, steering her away from clusters of people, tightening her grip every time someone says, "We heard about your father…"

Isla doesn't respond.

She doesn't give anyone the satisfaction of watching her flinch.

At the reception, champagne glasses clink, and strings of light glow overhead. People congratulate Isla in warm, eager voices that blur together. The competition director praises her artistry. Someone asks about her future career.

Isla nods. Smiles. Thanks them.

All the while, she feels Alisa's tension humming beside her like a warning.

Finally, as the room begins to thin and the clamor softens, Isla slips toward the side corridor leading to the exit.

Alisa catches up instantly.

"We go now," she says, too sharp to be merely a suggestion.

Isla pauses near a framed poster listing past winners, names that had become legends. She touches the edge of the frame, grounding herself, then looks at her mother.

"What did you mean," Isla asks, "when you said it's about what happens next?"

Alisa's eyes harden. "Don't ask questions here."

Isla's mouth tightens. "He's dead. That's the only fact you've given me."

"That's enough, for now." Alisa's voice is brittle.

Isla studies her mother's face, the tightness around her mouth, the strain in her eyes. Alisa MacLaren does not panic easily. She doesn't *do* messy. Everything in Isla's life, every lesson, every schedule, every decision, has been arranged by Alisa like a masterpiece under glass.

So why does Alisa look like the glass is about to shatter?

"Is the money going to stop?" Isla asks quietly.

Alisa freezes.

For half a second, the silence between them is loud.

Then Alisa's face flashes with indignation. "Is that what you think this is about?"

Isla doesn't flinch. "Isn't it?"

Alisa's eyes go glossy with rage or grief or both. "That money was owed."

"Owed," Isla repeats, tasting the word. "For what? For leaving?"

Alisa's jaw clenches. "For the life he destroyed. For promises he broke. For—"

Alisa stops herself, swallowing the rest.

For the first time, Isla wonders if there are more details in Alisa's history with Keir than she's been allowed to know. Isla knew the official story: the rock star father who walked away from his wife and daughter. The furious mother who rebuilt a life, the monthly payments like hush money disguised as support.

But there were always more shadows behind official stories.

"Did you love him?" Isla asks before she can stop herself.

Alisa's eyes snap to hers. "Years ago."

That is answer enough.

They move toward the side exit, away from the reception, away from the remaining well-wishers. Alisa keeps her hand on Isla's back like a guide and a guard, pushing her forward.

Outside, the air is cool and damp, laced with the scent of the ocean carried inland. The night should have felt victorious, the winning medal around her neck secured, the future cracking open into possibility.

Instead, the moment the door opens, the world surges at them.

Lights. Shouts. Cameras.

"Isla! Isla MacLaren, this way!"

"Is it true about your father?"

"Keir MacLaren is dead. Do you have a statement?"

"Did you know before your performance?"

"Was your piece dedicated to him?"

Microphones shove toward Isla's face. A bright light shines from a camera almost in her face. The. press formed a semi-circle outside the venue, waiting like predators who'd scented blood.

Isla's heart beat once, hard.

Alisa grabs Isla's hand and pulls her forward. "Keep your head down," she hisses. "Don't say anything."

Isla's jaw tightens.

She hates this.

She hates the way her father could still take center stage in her life without ever being present. She hates that in the same night she won something she had earned with her own hands and her own discipline, the world decided the headline would be about him.

Keir MacLaren.

A reporter shoves closer. "Isla—were you close with him?"

Close?

Isla almost laughs. The absurdity of it.

Alisa pushes harder, dragging Isla toward the waiting limo. A security guard tries to hold the press back, but the crowd surges. Someone calls Isla's name again, loud and insistent, as if saying it enough times would crack her open.

Isla keeps moving, face composed, eyes forward, posture flawless.

A microphone is shoved in her face, the reporter stepping alongside her.

She stumbles a half step.

Alisa's grip tightens like a vise. "Move," she snarls.

They reach the limo. The driver holds the door open. Alisa shoves Isla inside first, then followed, slamming the door shut behind them with a finality that muffled the shouting outside.

The interior is dark and cool, smelling faintly of leather and expensive cologne.

The limo lurches forward.

Isla stares out the tinted window as the press dissolves into streaks of light and movement. Her reflection stares back at her, perfect hair, perfect makeup, a medal glinting coldly at her throat.

A winner.

A daughter of a dead rock star.

Beside her, Alisa turns sharply, rage colliding with fear in her expression.

"I told you," Alisa growls, "we needed to leave earlier."

Isla doesn't look away from the window. Her voice is quiet, controlled, cutting.

"He left first."

Alisa's breath catches. For a moment, Isla thinks her mother might say something cruel, something honest.

Instead, Alisa stares at her, eyes bright with something she refuses to name.

"You don't understand," Alisa says.

Isla finally turns her head. "Then explain it."

Alisa opens her mouth.

Closes it.

Her gaze flicks to Isla's medal, as if even that had become dangerous.

"We'll talk when we get home," Alisa says tightly. "Not here."

Isla's lips thin. "You mean when you can control the narrative?"

Alisa's hand curls into a fist in her lap. "I mean when it's safe."

Safe.

The word makes Isla's skin prickle.

She leans back against the leather seat, posture still elegant even in exhaustion. Outside, the streetlights slip past in an even rhythm. The limo's motion is steady, controlled, unlike the night.

Isla presses two fingers lightly against the cold of her medal, grounding herself.

She won.

That is real.

Keir MacLaren's death is also real, apparently.

But Isla refuses to let that reality rewrite her own.

He had chosen absence.

He had chosen everything but her.

He doesn't get to claim a place in her heart now just because the world wants a tragic story.

Isla closes her eyes briefly, listening to the hum of tires on pavement, feeling the weight of the medal at her throat.

Somewhere beyond the tinted glass, the ocean keeps moving, indifferent.

And somewhere, far away, a man who has never been a father has died, leaving behind consequences Isla does not yet understand.

CHAPTER 2

allum Fraser's cell phone rings with an insistence that breaks the quiet of the car somewhere outside Glasgow, past the last strip of fast-food lights, past the exit that smells like diesel and boiled peanuts, into that long stretch of highway where the world turns into lanes and sky and the steady hum of tires. The radio is low, not music, never music when he's trying not to think, just voices filling the air without asking anything of him.

His phone buzzes against the console.

He glances down. Unknown number.

He should ignore it. He's due in Dumfries by late afternoon for soundcheck, and he's already behind. But the number flashes again, insistent, and something in his gut tightens as if it recognizes trouble before his brain does.

He answers through the steering wheel button. "Yeah?"

A pause. Not the breathless pause of someone lost, not the awkward pause of a wrong number. A pause that feels… careful.

"Mr. Fraser?" a man asks.

Callum's grip tightens. "Speaking."

"This is Andrew Bell of Bell & Morrison. Keir MacLaren's attorney." The voice is polished, controlled, Scottish, clipped, trained to deliver bad news without being stained by it. "I'm afraid I have some very difficult news."

Callum's chest constricts as if a hand has closed around his ribs. "About what?"

"Keir MacLaren."

The road wavers. His vision narrows down to the white lines and the strip of gray pavement ahead.

"What about him?" Callum hears himself ask. He doesn't like his own voice; it sounds too calm, too steady, as if he's pretending this is a normal call.

The pause returns. Longer.

"I'm very sorry to tell you that Mr. MacLaren passed away late last night. It appears to have been a heart attack."

The world doesn't explode. It tilts.

For a second, Callum thinks the words didn't land. That the sentence slid past him without meaning. Heart attack. Passed away. Late last night.

"No," he says, so quietly he almost can't hear it over the tires. "No. That's not possible."

"I'm very sorry."

Callum pulls the car onto the shoulder without signaling. Gravel crunches beneath the tires. The car shudders, then stills. He stares straight ahead at a smear of sky and the blur of trees, hands locked on the wheel like it's the only thing keeping him upright.

"You've got the wrong man," he says. "You must."

"I assure you, Mr. Fraser—"

"I talked to him three days ago." The words come out sharp. "He was, he was fine. He was complaining about my setlist and telling me to sleep more. He doesn't just—"

Die.

The word jams in his throat like a bone.

"We've confirmed his identity," Bell says gently. "Emergency services responded, but he was pronounced dead at the scene."

Callum's forehead drops against the steering wheel. The horn gives a short, pathetic sound, like the car is mocking him.

Keir is dead.

The man who had been more than a mentor. More than a bandmate. More than a legend. The man who had been – when Callum was fourteen, and the world had decided he was a lost cause – his lifeline.

Callum breathes in once, but it doesn't feel like air. It feels like emptiness.

Bell keeps talking, words turning into mush, arrangements, immediate matters, the estate, the need for Callum to return as soon as possible.

"Home," Bell says at one point, and that one word slices through Callum with a clean, ruthless edge.

Home.

Not the flat his mother had moved him into when she remarried and decided she needed her new husband more than she needed her son.

Not the boys' school with its locked doors, rules, and quiet cruelty.

Home was stone walls and cold hallways and a fire always burning in the hearth. Home was Keir MacLaren swearing at the kettle and strumming a guitar at midnight like sleep was optional. Home was being hauled out of a place that smelled like bleach and punishment, and being told, without softness, without pity—

You're coming with me.

"You understand?" Bell asks.

Callum lifts his head slowly. His eyes burn. He swipes at his face, furious at the betrayal of tears.

"Yeah," he croaks. "I understand."

"I'll be at the castle when you arrive," Bell says. "There are legal matters we must discuss. And…someone else."

Callum frowns. "Someone else?"

Bell hesitates. "We'll speak when you get here, Mr. Fraser."

The line goes dead.

Callum sits in the silence, as if he's waiting for the solicitor to call back and correct himself.

Keir is dead.

The sentence repeats in his head, useless, impossible, obscene. For the last week, he'd been on the road performing at different pubs, playing and doing what he loved.

And now he would be returning to an empty castle.

A truck roars past on the highway, wind buffeting the car. The world keeps moving. The world is disrespectful like that.

Callum laughs once, a short, broken sound. "Fuck," he whispers.

He turns the car around.

He drives like a man chasing a ghost.

Hours compress. Gas stations blur into one another, bright aisles, bitter coffee, fluorescent lights that make his skin look sick. He doesn't remember eating. He remembers buying something wrapped in plastic, taking two bites, and throwing it away because it tasted like cardboard and grief.

As the miles pass, his mind returns to the crash that changed his life.

Callum is twelve again, sitting on the floor of a living room that smells like lemon polish and his father's aftershave. His mother's hands shake around a glass she never drinks from. The news says private plane, crash and burn, no survivors. His father, who had finally made enough money to buy the kind of freedom men brag about, had learned to fly like it was a trophy.

Callum remembers the way people said, *tragic, senseless,* with their sad eyes and their softer voices, like tragedy was a thing to be admired.

He remembers that after, everything got quieter. His mother got sharper. Less patient. More tired. And then she remarried, as if love was a doorway out of grief, and Callum became the thing that didn't fit in the new life.

By fourteen, Callum is made entirely of rage.

Rage at his father for leaving. Rage at his mother for moving on. Rage at himself for still wanting anyone to choose him.

He gets into trouble, real trouble. Not childish rebellion, not scraped knees and foul language. Trouble that lands him in court. Trouble that his mother can't stand to see in her new husband's house.

So she sends him away.

The boys' school is all stone and discipline and silence. It smells like damp wool, bleach, and hopelessness. The staff speaks in clipped commands. The older boys learn where to hide bruises. Callum learns to punch first. To keep his back to the wall. To sleep with one ear open.

He tells himself no one is coming.

Then one day, the headmaster calls him to the office.

A man stands there, tall, broad-shouldered, hair too long, eyes too bright. The staff treats him with a strange kind of respect and admiration, someone famous. His father's best friend.

Keir MacLaren.

Callum recognized him instantly from the time he'd spent with his father, from posters, from television, from the way people said his name like it was a dare. A rock god. A disaster. A brilliant man who doesn't belong to rules.

Keir looks at Callum like he is evaluating a guitar that might be worth fixing.

"So you're the troublemaker," Keir says.

Callum lifts his chin. "I don't think so. What are you doing here?"

Keir smiles, sharp as a blade. "I'm getting you out of this place."

Callum doesn't believe him.

Not until Keir signs papers with a scrawl that looks like a signature and a warning.

Not until Keir walks him out past the locked gates, tosses his duffel bag into the boot of his car, and says, "Get in."

No lecture. No pity. No promises he couldn't keep.

Just action.

Structure.

Choice.

Keir had chosen him.

And now Keir is gone.

Callum's hands ache on the steering wheel as the memory snaps back into the present.

The sky is the color of steel when he turns onto the narrow road that winds through heather and stone fences. Fog clings to the hills like breath. The land feels ancient and watchful, the kind of place that remembers everything and forgives nothing.

Then the castle appears. Home for the last ten years. A place where he'd found his passion and become a man.

Gray stone rising out of mist, stubborn and imposing, like it's holding its ground against time itself. Ivy climbs one wall, uninvited. Windows stare out over the land like dark eyes.

Callum's throat tightens so hard, it hurts.

This place, these walls, are home.

Not the place he was born. Not the life he lost when his father's plane burned. Not the tidy world his mother built with another man and another set of rules.

Home is here. In the echoing halls where Keir's laugh had bounced. In the music room where the guitars sit like sleeping animals. In the kitchen, where Keir had sworn at the kettle and made terrible tea and acted as if rules were optional but loyalty was not.

At the gate, paparazzi are gathered. A makeshift memorial stands there with flowers scattered everywhere. Left by hundreds of fans. All for the man who is now gone.

Callum's chest aches with unshed tears for the man who'd saved him.

When the gate opens, he pulls into the drive and cuts the engine. For a moment, he can't move. His hands are locked on the wheel again, like letting go will make it real.

He swallows hard. Forces himself out of the car.

The cold air hits his face like a slap. The scent of wet stone and peat and distant smoke fills his lungs. He stands there looking up at the castle, and grief comes in a wave so strong, it nearly drops him to his knees.

Keir is dead.

The words still don't fit.

Callum crosses the gravel, boots crunching, and shoves the heavy front door open.

The familiar creak answers him.

Inside, the air is colder than he expects. Quiet. Too quiet.

The castle without Keir feels like a body without a heartbeat. Before you would have heard rock music resounding through the halls, laughter and food, and the occasional party. But now it's silent.

Callum steps into the entry hall and stops. His gaze sweeps over the familiar details: the worn runner rug, the old portraits staring down with judgment, the coat rack where Keir always tossed his jacket instead of hanging it properly.

Callum's mouth opens. "I'm back," he says automatically. But this time, there is no response.

His voice echoes back at him.

No reply.

Memories hit like fists.

Keir in this hall, arms folded, furious after Callum showed up drunk at seventeen, knuckles split and lip bleeding from a fight Callum couldn't even remember starting.

You want to stay here? You follow my rules. You get your head on straight. You stop trying to die.

Callum had laughed then, bitter and defiant. "Why do you care?"

Keir had stared at him a long moment, then said, "Because you're here. Because your father would want me to kick your butt and keep you from dying."

As if that was enough.

It had been.

Another memory: Callum at the kitchen table, trying to read a contract with words too small and too many pages, ready to throw it across the room.

Keir had yanked it back. "Read it. Every word. Don't let anyone take your life because you were too lazy to learn."

"Why are you doing this?" Callum had demanded.

Keir had shrugged. "Someone should've done it for me."

Callum drops his bag by the door and moves deeper into the castle, touching things without thinking, stone walls, the banister worn smooth by centuries, the edge of a table scarred with old burns and old laughter.

The music room door is half open.

He pushes it wider.

Dust motes float in the weak light. The fireplace is cold. Keir's favorite guitar rests on its stand, strings slack, silent.

Callum crosses the room, knees suddenly unsteady. He sits on the piano bench as if the weight of his body has finally caught up to him. He stares at the guitar until his vision blurs.

"You didn't tell me," he whispers into the quiet. "You didn't… tell me how to do this without you."

His throat tightens, and grief claws up, sharp and ugly. Callum presses his fist into his chest like he can push the pain down where it belongs.

Orphans weren't supposed to get second chances.

He'd already lost his father at twelve, lost him to fire and wreckage and a headline that said *tragic accident.* He'd lost his mother in every way that mattered when she sent him away at fourteen, choosing a new life over the son who didn't fit.

Keir had been the man who'd filled that hole.

Not gently. Not with sentimental speeches.

With presence. With discipline. With a place at the table and rules that meant someone cared whether Callum lived or died.

Now that is gone.

Footsteps echo in the corridor, measured and cautious.

Callum wipes his face with the heel of his hand and forces his shoulders back. He refuses to look like a child who's been abandoned. Though right now his chest aches so hard that he fears he is having a heart attack.

A man stands in the doorway, mid-fifties, neat suit, eyes tired.

"Mr. Fraser," he says softly. "Andrew Bell. We spoke earlier."

Callum nods once. His voice is rough. "Yeah."

"I'm sorry for your loss."

Callum's jaw clenches. "So am I."

Bell's gaze flicks to the guitar, then back. "We should talk. There are arrangements and legal matters."

Callum stands, legs stiff, and follows Bell into the study.

The study looks wrong. Keir's absence is everywhere, an unfinished glass on the desk, papers stacked haphazardly, a jacket draped over a chair like Keir might come back to claim it.

Bell closes the door behind them. The click sounds too final.

"Please sit," Bell says.

Callum doesn't want to sit. Sitting feels like surrender. He does it anyway, because Keir taught him you could be hurt and still be smart.

Bell opens a folder. "Keir MacLaren's will is…straightforward in some ways and complicated in others."

"Just tell me what I need to do," Callum says tightly.

"You are the executor." Bell studies him for a moment, then speaks carefully. "But, there is a matter of next of kin."

Callum's eyes narrow. "Next of kin?"

Bell clears his throat. "Keir MacLaren had a daughter."

The sentence doesn't land. It detonates.

Callum's body goes rigid. "What?"

That can't be possible. He'd never mentioned having a child of his own.

"A daughter," Bell repeats gently, as if Callum might not have heard English the first time. "Isla MacLaren. She is, legally, his child. His heir."

Callum stares at him.

"No," he says, voice low and dangerous. "No. That's not possible."

Why hadn't the press mentioned her?

"It is," Bell says. "Keir acknowledged her. Paternity is documented. She is his sole biological child."

Callum's hands curl into fists so tight, his knuckles ache.

Keir never talked about a daughter.

Not once.

Keir had told Callum about addiction and regret and mistakes made on tour. He'd confessed to failures with brutal honesty, like he believed the only way to survive was to drag the truth into the light and stare it down.

But a daughter?

"You're telling me," Callum says slowly, each word edged with disbelief, "that the man who raised me had a child he never mentioned?"

Bell nods. "I understand this is a shock."

Shock doesn't cover it.

It feels like betrayal.

Like Keir had kept a locked room in the castle and never trusted Callum with the key.

"She's coming here?" Callum asks, voice flat.

"Yes," Bell says. "She's currently in the United States. She has been informed of Keir's death and will be arriving soon. We'll need her presence for certain legal formalities."

Callum's stomach turns.

A stranger walking through these halls.

A daughter stepping into a life Keir never spoke of.

And Callum – who had been rescued at fourteen, felt like he was twelve years old again, staring at a television screen while someone says *no survivors.*

His voice comes out rough. "Why didn't he tell me?"

Bell's expression softens with something like regret. "I can't speak to Keir's reasons. But I can tell you the will includes provisions that suggest...he expected conflict."

"Conflict," Callum repeats, bitter.

Bell glances at the folder. "The castle. The estate. The rights. Keir's holdings are significant."

Callum's gaze drifts to the stone walls, the shelves, the desk where Keir had sat pretending paperwork didn't bore him. This place isn't just property. It's proof. It's belonging.

The only real home Callum has ever had. And losing the castle would be crushing.

"You're saying she gets the castle," Callum says quietly. "But he said I was going to inherit the castle."

"I'm saying," Bell replies, "that the will acknowledges her legal claim. And that Keir also made arrangements for you."

Callum snaps his eyes back. "Arrangements?"

Bell's mouth tightens. "Yes. Keir was...very clear about your importance to him."

Callum goes silent, the words refusing to come. Because that's the part that hurts worst, Keir had cared. Callum knows he had. He knows it in every rule Keir enforced, every late-night talk, every time Keir showed up when no one else did.

And yet Keir had still kept this secret.

Bell continues, "There will be a meeting when Miss MacLaren arrives. Until then, I recommend you rest."

Rest.

As if Callum can sleep in a castle that suddenly feels like it might be taken from him.

As if he can close his eyes without seeing fire and wreckage, without hearing Keir's voice telling him to get his head on straight, without feeling the cold hollow of being orphaned, again.

Callum stands abruptly from the couch, his balance teetering.

Bell looks up. "Mr. Fraser—"

Callum's voice is raw. "Tell me one thing."

"Yes?"

"Did Keir…did he ever look for her?"

Bell hesitates. "I don't know. But based on financial records, he sent regular payments to Miss MacLaren and her mother."

Callum flinches. Regular payments.

Keir had always been good at sending money in the right direction. It was easier than showing up. Easier than being seen.

Callum turns away, staring at the window where the fog presses against the glass. The land outside is gray and ancient and indifferent.

"A daughter," Callum says again, like saying it might make it make sense.

Bell's voice is gentle. "She'll be here soon."

Callum closes his eyes.

He can handle grief. He can handle loss. He can handle rage.

But this, this feels like the start of something else entirely.

Keir is gone, and with him the one person who held Callum's world together.

Now the castle waits, cold and watchful. And even that could be taken from him.

And somewhere across an ocean, a woman who shares Keir's

blood is coming here, into Callum's home, into Callum's life, carrying a claim Callum never saw coming.

Callum opens his eyes, jaw clenched.

He isn't just grieving.

He's bracing for war.

And the worst part is, he doesn't even know who the enemy is yet.

"I'm not giving up the castle. It's mine."

CHAPTER 3

By the time the castle comes into view, Isla MacLaren is operating on rage, caffeine, and stubborn refusal.

The drive from the airport has blurred into gray roads and mist and her mother's relentless voice. Twelve hours of flying, three connections, one merciless overnight layover, and Alisa MacLaren has not stopped talking once, not to rest, not to think, not to breathe.

"He ruined everything," Alisa says from the back seat of the hired car, her tone sharp and precise, as if she's delivering a lecture instead of reliving a marriage. "Absolutely everything. Do you know how humiliating it was, being married to a man like that?"

Isla stares out the window, jaw tight, watching stone fences slide past in the fog.

"You've told me," Isla says quietly.

"And now," Alisa continues, unfazed, "after all these years, he dies and leaves us with this mess. Typical. Absolutely typical."

Isla closes her eyes.

She knows the story. She has always known the story. Her

mother has told it with variations, depending on the mood and the audience.

Keir MacLaren: the brilliant musician. The addict. The cheater. The man who chose drugs and groupies and chaos over responsibility. The man who abandoned his wife and infant daughter and disappeared into fame.

Isla had grown up with that version of him, polished sharp and repeated until it felt like fact carved in stone.

And yet—

Even bad people can do some good.

The thought irritates her, but it won't leave.

Keir never sent birthday cards. Never showed up. Never called. Never asked to hear her play. Isla has never seen his face in real life, never heard his voice without a screen between them.

But the money came. Every month. Without fail.

The best teachers. The best instruments. The best schools. The travel. The competitions.

Luxury.

Comfort.

Opportunity.

Her childhood was not one of struggle. It was one of pressure, expectation, and polish.

That money made her life possible.

And now Alisa is already counting it again.

"I just want to know what he left," Alisa says. "After everything, he owes us that much."

Isla opens her eyes, anger flaring sharp and sudden. "He's dead."

Alisa waves a hand. "And?"

The word lands wrong.

Isla turns, finally meeting her mother's gaze in the reflection of the window. Alisa's face is tight with exhaustion and resentment, and something else Isla doesn't want to name: anticipation.

"He's been dead less than forty-eight hours," Isla says. "Could you not—"

"Not what?" Alisa snaps. "Be practical? We need to know where we stand."

Where we stand.

As if grief is a financial position.

Isla looks away again, heat crawling up her neck. "You're not even curious about him."

Alisa scoffs. "I know everything I need to know."

That, Isla realizes, is the problem.

The castle emerges out of the mist like something half-forgotten, half-dared into existence. Gray stone rises from the land, ancient and imposing, ivy crawling along its walls as if trying to reclaim it inch by inch.

It's not romantic in the way Isla expected.

It's heavier.

Older.

A crowd of expectant paparazzi stands waiting in front of the gate. The flashes go off as the car waits for the gate to open. Every newspaper she'd seen in the airport had the headlines that Keir MacLaren was dead.

Never to sing again or play his guitar or even the keyboard he kept on stage. Never to get the chance to know his daughter.

The limo pulls into the gravel drive, tires crunching loudly in the silence. Isla steps out, stiff and sore, jet lag pressing behind her eyes like a bruise.

Cold air hits her in the face, and she breathes in the Scottish air.

This is where he lived.

This is where he chose to be.

The thought stings more than she expects.

"Hello," a lady in a white uniform says. "Follow me."

Quickly, the maid ushers them into the castle.

"It's a pleasure to meet you. Ma'am, you'll be in the east wing.

Your mother right across the hall from you. Tea will be served at four p.m. The butler will bring up your luggage. My name is Matilda. If you need anything at all, don't hesitate to ring me."

She leads them up the stairs to their bedrooms.

Inside, the castle is dim and cool, the air smelling faintly of stone, wood smoke, and something masculine, leather, perhaps. Isla's footsteps echo too loudly on the floor, her heels sounding foreign and intrusive.

A sense of feeling out of place creeps over her. Her father's house.

"Mr. Bell would like to speak to you whenever you're ready. He's in Mr. Keir's study on the first floor."

The maid disappears, and Isla sinks onto her bed. She glances around the room, a feeling of despair fills her. Why is this the first time she's ever been in her father's house?

She has to get out of here.

Opening the door, she hurries back downstairs, her exhaustion momentarily forgotten. A feeling of foreboding sends her fleeing.

Downstairs, she sees her mother walking into the study. Sigh. Of course, she goes straight to the study. She wants to know what they will inherit.

The solicitor greets them, polite, careful, already measuring, and ushers Alisa into conversation. Isla drifts away, uninterested in legal logistics and wills and estates she never asked for.

But not her mother. She's all about the inheritance, and that irks Isla.

She needs space. A place to escape from the despair and hopelessness filling her. In a cruel twist of fate, she will never know her father.

She wanders down a corridor, then another, the castle unfolding in quiet wings and turns. Portraits line the walls, stern faces, judgmental eyes. She wonders briefly if Keir ever felt watched here.

A door stands ajar at the end of a hallway.

Isla pushes it open without thinking.

She assumes it's staff space. Storage. A back corridor she shouldn't be in. All she was looking for was a place to escape this massive building. A door to the outside.

Instead, she collides with a solid body.

"Oof—!"

She stumbles forward, hands coming up instinctively, palms landing on a man's chest.

A very warm, very solid chest. The smell of woodsmoke and something alluring teases her nose. A ripple shudders through her body.

Strong hands grip her arms, steadying her before she can fall. Isla jerks back, breath sharp, heart slamming into her ribs.

"What the hell?" she snaps.

The man in front of her is tall. Broad-shouldered. Dressed in an emerald kilt that has all the regalia. His socks come to his knees, his tartan crosses his chest. His hair is dark and slightly too long, his jaw rough with stubble.

He does not look like staff.

He looks like trouble.

"You walked into me," he says flatly.

Isla bristles. "You were standing in the middle of a hallway."

"Because it's my hallway."

She blinks. "Excuse me?"

His gaze flicks over her, expensive jacket, designer heels, posture sharpened by years of being watched, and something hardens in his eyes.

"Oh," he says. "You must be her."

Her temper flares instantly. "Her who?"

"The ghost," he says coolly. "The absentee daughter."

The words hit like a glass of ice water.

Isla straightens. "And he was an absentee father," she snaps, because, apparently, this is what they're doing now, throwing assumptions like knives.

"I don't believe you," he replies.

Her mouth falls open. "What did you just say?"

He folds his arms. "You show up late. Only when he's dead. Wander where you don't belong. Act like everyone should move out of your way."

Isla laughs, sharp and incredulous. "And you are...what? A groupie? A friend who never left?"

His jaw tightens. "Careful."

"Why?" Isla shoots back. "I assume you're one of his, what do you call yourselves, proteges? Fans? People who benefit from orbiting him?"

"That's rich," he says, eyes darkening. "Coming from someone who benefited without ever showing up."

Her pulse spikes.

"I didn't abandon him," Isla snaps. "He abandoned me."

His gaze flickers. Something like pain flashes there before hardening into anger.

"You think that makes you special?" he says quietly. "You think you're the only one he didn't show up for?"

Isla takes a step closer, fueled by exhaustion and grief and twelve hours of listening to her mother tear a man apart. "You don't get to judge me. After all, I never spoke to him."

"And you don't get to waltz in here like this place is a hotel suite you forgot you booked," he fires back.

They're standing too close now.

Isla smells him, soap, leather, something warm and human. Awareness sparks low in her stomach, unwelcome and confusing.

She hates that her body notices.

She hates that his eyes linger a second too long.

"Who are you?" she demands.

He hesitates.

Just a fraction.

"Someone who actually knew him," he says.

The words sting more than any insult.

Isla swallows. "You knew a version of him."

His mouth curves into something bitter. "And you knew nothing."

"Oh, you are so right," she says.

Footsteps sound behind them.

"Isla!"

Alisa's voice cuts through the tension like a blade. Isla turns, relief and irritation tangling together.

"There you are," Alisa says, sweeping toward them. Her eyes flick over the man with quick assessment. "And who is this?"

Callum stiffens.

Isla answers before he can. "Apparently, someone who thinks I don't belong here."

Alisa's lips thin. "We are Keir MacLaren's family."

The man's gaze sharpens. "That's debatable."

Alisa bristles. "Excuse me?"

He looks directly at Isla's mother now, and Isla sees something in his expression, contained grief, tightly leashed fury.

"He raised me," the man says. "He chose me. He loved me, and I loved him."

Alisa scoffs. "That doesn't make you family."

Callum's hands curl into fists at his sides. "Funny. He never chose you."

The silence that follows is electric.

Isla feels caught between them, heart pounding, emotions flaring in every direction at once.

"This conversation is over," Alisa snaps. "We didn't come here to be insulted by—"

"By someone who stayed?" Callum interrupts. "Someone who showed up when it mattered?"

Isla steps forward without thinking. "Stop."

They both look at her.

"I didn't ask for this," Isla says, voice tight. "I didn't ask to be born. I didn't ask to be ignored. And I didn't ask to be dragged halfway across the world to stand in his house while strangers tell me who he was."

Callum studies her then, really studies her, and for the first time, his anger wavers.

For a split second, Isla sees something else in his eyes.

Recognition.

Then it's gone.

"Welcome to the club," he says coolly. "The Keir MacLaren family club."

Alisa exhales sharply. "We'll be speaking with the solicitor now."

She grips Isla's arm and pulls her away.

Isla doesn't look back.

She feels him watching her.

Her pulse refuses to settle.

Her anger burns bright and messy and unresolved.

Her first impression of whoever the hell he is, is catastrophic.

And the worst part?

Somewhere beneath the fury and grief and exhaustion, Isla is painfully aware of one thing she does not want to examine.

This man, this stranger who loved her father, matters.

And that complicates everything.

CHAPTER 4

Callum has never hated a crowd the way he despises this one.

They line the stone path to the chapel, spilling across the castle grounds as if this is a pilgrimage instead of a funeral. Black coats and dark sunglasses. Camera lenses peeking from behind scarves. Fans clutching vinyl albums and handwritten signs, faces reverent, tear-streaked, ecstatic.

Some of them are singing.

Not recorded. Not polished.

Keir's songs, off-key, heartfelt, uninvited, float through the cold air like a wake that refuses to end.

Callum stands near the chapel doors, hands shoved deep into his coat pockets, wearing his finest kilt, jaw locked so tightly, his temples ache. Every note feels like a theft.

This isn't theirs.

Keir was theirs on stage. On tape. On the internet. On the radio.

But this, this is supposed to be private.

Instead, it's a spectacle.

Celebrities drift past, each one carefully composed in grief. Actors Keir once dated. Musicians who once fought with him, loved him, nearly killed him with excess, and then laughed about it years later. Producers and industry men who owe entire careers to Keir's musical instincts.

Media vans idle down the road, satellite dishes angled skyward like vultures waiting for the signal.

This is not a goodbye.

It's a canonization.

Inside the chapel, the air is thick with incense, reverence, and expectation. Cameras are banned, but Callum knows better. Someone always finds a way. There will be leaked footage, whispered quotes, headlines already half-written.

He takes a seat near the front, close enough to see everything, far enough to avoid the worst of the stares.

The casket is closed.

Thank God.

Keir MacLaren, reduced to wood and silence, would break something in Callum that he isn't sure would come back.

The service begins the way all services for famous men begin, with stories carefully orchestrated for public consumption.

Keir the genius.

Keir the visionary.

Keir the man who changed music forever.

One speaker after another steps forward, each polishing the legend until it gleams. A producer talks about Keir's ear, his fearlessness, his generosity.

"He would give you the shirt off his back," the man says, voice thick with emotion. "He loved deeply. He lived fully."

Callum's fingers curl into fists.

Would he?

Keir had given Callum a home. Structure. Discipline. A second chance when no one else bothered to see one.

But Keir had also vanished from entire parts of his own life.

Another speaker follows, this one sanctimonious, self-important, clearly enjoying the sound of his own voice.

"Keir's devotion to family was unparalleled," the man declares. "He believed in connection above all else."

Callum's jaw tightens.

That's when he looks at Isla and his heart cracks.

She sits in the second row beside her mother, rigid as a drawn blade. Her black dress is sharp and tailored, with no softness to it. Her posture is perfect. Controlled. Her face is calm in the way only someone who has learned not to expect comfort can be calm.

She has not cried.

Alisa MacLaren dabs at her eyes with a handkerchief, grief neat and measured. Isla stares straight ahead, unmoving, like she's enduring something rather than participating.

Something in Callum twists.

The speaker continues, droning on about Keir's warmth, his capacity for love.

This is bullshit.

Callum shifts, anger coiling tight in his chest. He knows Keir's flaws. He lived with them. He forgave them. He worked around them.

But turning the man into a saint?

That feels like a lie too far.

The speaker finally steps down. The officiant hesitates, scanning the room, preparing to continue.

That's when Isla stands.

The movement is so sudden it sends a ripple through the pews. Heads turn. Whispers spark instantly.

Callum's breath catches.

What the hell is she doing?

She steps into the aisle without looking at anyone, heels clicking softly against stone. For a split second, Callum thinks she's going to speak, say something sharp, something reckless.

Instead, she turns toward the piano.

A low murmur rolls through the chapel.

Isla sits at the bench.

No introduction. No permission.

She places her hands on the keys.

Callum recognizes the posture immediately, the way her shoulders settle, the way her fingers hover like they're deciding whether to strike or soothe.

This isn't performance.

This is confession.

She starts to play.

It's one of Keir's songs.

Callum knows it instantly, a crowd favorite, usually loud and electric, all swagger and deflection.

Isla guts it.

She strips it down to melody and bone, slowing it until every note aches. The piano doesn't try to fill the space, it exposes it. Where Keir's version hid pain behind bravado, hers drags the pain into the light and forces it to stay there.

Then she sings.

Her voice isn't big.

It's clear. Bare. Unforgiving. The words are her own to her father's melody.

* * *

They say you lit up every room
Had the world hanging on your sound
Funny how a man that loud
Never made it back to town
Your face was on every magazine
Mine was pressed against the glass

> *Everyone got memories*
> *I just got the cash*

* * *

> *I never knew you*
> *Not the man they sing about*
> *You were always just a shadow*
> *On the edge of every crowd*
> *They tell me I should feel the loss*
> *Like I'm supposed to cry on cue*
> *But I can't miss what I never had*
> *'Cause I never knew you*

A SHARP INTAKE of breath ripples through the chapel. Callum's chest tightens.

* * *

> *Other children had their daddies*
> *Hands to catch them when they fell*
> *I learned early not to wait*
> *Not to ask. Turns out absence has a way*
> *Of making you hate what you never had*

HER VOICE DOESN'T CRACK.

* * *

> *I never knew you*
> *Not your hands, not your truth*
> *I never knew your promises*
> *Or which ones you'd refuse*
> *They say blood is everything*

Like it makes us somehow true
But all it ever gave me
Was a man I never knew

ISLA'S HANDS strike the keys again, harder now.

* * *

They say you would've loved me
If you'd stayed a little while
Guess the encore mattered more than I

* * *

A WOMAN in the front row begins to cry openly. Isla doesn't look up.

* * *

So don't tell me what you meant to be
Or who you were inside
I don't miss what I never had
I just learned how to survive

* * *

I never knew you
And I stopped pretending I did
I mourned you years ago
When I was just a kid
I never knew you

* * *

So don't ask me to forgive
You got the songs, the fame, the love
I got the life I had to live
So sing your praises, raise a glass
Say you never had a clue
But when I walk away from here
I'll still say—I never knew you

ISLA PLAYS the final phrase and stops, abruptly, brutally, cutting the song off mid-breath.

The silence is violent.

She stands.

Turns to face the room.

Her voice is calm. Steady. Deadly honest.

"He loved music," she says. "He just didn't love being a father."

Gasps explode through the chapel. She walks over to the casket and softly sings a cappella.

"And now I will never know you."

Chaos ignites instantly.

Callum feels like he's been punched in the chest.

This isn't a tribute.

This is an indictment.

Whispers surge. Shock ricochets. Alisa hisses Isla's name, horror etched across her face. Somewhere, someone drops a program. Callum can almost *hear* the headlines forming.

Rock Legend's Daughter Shatters Funeral

Estranged Child Calls Out Father's Failure

Keir MacLaren's Myth Cracks in Public

Callum can't move.

Anger floods him first, hot, immediate.

How dare she?

How dare she stand there and reduce Keir to his worst failure? How dare she dismiss everything Keir was, everything he gave, everything he saved?

And then—

Something else cuts through.

Because she isn't lying.

Keir loved music more than sobriety. More than stability. More than showing up when it mattered most.

Callum knows that truth intimately.

Isla turns and walks back to her seat without looking at anyone. Not the officiant. Not her mother.

Not him.

He could feel the anger rolling off her, the rage, the hurt. He could see the tears brimming in her eyes. Pulling her shoulders back, she sank down and released a shaky breath.

The service limped forward, but it never recovered from her performance. People are shaken. The sanctimony is gone, stripped bare by one woman and a piano.

Callum remains seated long after it ends.

Long after people rise and whisper and rush outside, phones already out, grief already being monetized.

He stares at the piano.

At the space where Isla's hands had been.

He wants to hate her.

Instead, he feels wrecked.

Because she didn't just expose Keir.

She exposed the lie Callum has been living inside.

That love makes up for absence.

That forgiveness erases damage.

That some truths are better left unsaid.

Her song was devastating.

And beautiful.

And it proved something Callum was not ready to face yet.

Keir may not have loved being a father.

But his daughter?

She inherited the one thing Keir never lied about.

The music.

And Callum is standing far too close to the fire.

God, he wants to hear her play again. Because no matter the words, the notes spinning from her fingers were like magic. The artistry, the skill, even her voice, left him reeling from the music she created.

And yet, she'd just destroyed the man he loved. His second father.

CHAPTER 5

The party is wrong.

That is Isla MacLaren's first coherent thought as she steps into the long gallery of the castle and takes in the soft light, the circulating trays of champagne, the low murmur of conversation that hums with an energy entirely too alive for the day they've just endured.

Grief, apparently, has an expiration date. Right after the funeral. In the background, her father's music is softly playing.

She pauses just inside the doorway, spine straight, hands loosely clasped in front of her, as if posture alone can keep her emotions from spilling out. The echo of the chapel still rings in her ears, the brutal quiet after her song, the way the silence had pressed down like a held breath, like the world itself had stopped to listen.

She had expected outrage.

She had expected tears.

She had not expected the murmured approval that followed her down the aisle afterward. The whispered *brave, finally, someone said it,* offered by strangers who believed her pain belonged to them now.

She hadn't done it for them.

She had done it because she refused to lie. She refused to grieve for a man she'd never known.

And standing here now, watching people toast her father's life as though it were a successful album launch instead of a complicated wreckage, Isla feels something sharp and dangerous unfurl in her chest.

Pride.

She didn't fake grief.

She hadn't bowed her head and played the dutiful daughter. She hadn't softened herself to preserve a myth. She hadn't swallowed the truth to make other people comfortable.

Whatever comes next, she will not regret playing at his funeral.

"Smile," her mother murmurs beside her. "People are watching."

Isla doesn't turn. "Let them. What is there to be smiling about?"

Alisa MacLaren exhales sharply. "This is not the time to be difficult."

It's never the time. All her life, her mother just wanted her to obediently be the daughter she trained. The musician who was a concert pianist and not a rock star like her father.

Standing beside her mother, she scans the room instead.

The gallery stretches the length of the castle, ancient stone walls lined with portraits of people who look like they never asked permission to exist. Chandeliers cast a warm glow over polished floors. Servers move gracefully through clusters of mourners, offering champagne and delicate food no one seems to be eating.

Celebrities lean against centuries-old stone, grief tailored and elegant. Musicians gather in small knots, trading stories that sound suspiciously rehearsed. Industry people network even now, their sorrow compartmentalized and efficient.

Isla feels like a wrong note in a carefully rehearsed performance.

Softly, she slips away from her mother and drifts toward a tall window overlooking the green grass below. Outside, the fog has lifted just enough to reveal dark grass and bare trees, the land stretching outward like something ancient and watchful.

Her reflection stares back at her in the glass.

Composed. Controlled. Immaculate.

Inside, she feels emotionally raw.

"You did that on purpose."

The voice comes from behind her, low, controlled, threaded with fury held on a tight leash.

Isla closes her eyes briefly.

Of course, he followed her.

She turns slowly.

The man from earlier stands a few feet away, posture rigid, dark hair still damp from the mist outside. He's shed his coat and rolled his sleeves as if holding himself together has already cost him too much. Once again, he's wearing a kilt, which is ridiculously good-looking on him.

Up close, the awareness hits her again, unwanted and unwelcome. He is solid in a way that feels earned. Real. Not polished like the men circulating the room.

"What exactly did I do on purpose?" Isla asks coolly, knowing he's referring to her song at the funeral.

"You turned his funeral into a spectacle," he says. "Congratulations."

Her temper snaps to life. "It already was one."

"At least it was his spectacle and not yours."

"How?" she fires back. "Because they were glorifying him and making him into some perfect human being?"

His eyes flash. "Because they were mourning."

"I hardly call that mourning. It was more pretentious. Besides, do you think I care?"

He lets out a short, disbelieving laugh. "You humiliated him?"

By telling the truth, she thinks, but she doesn't say it yet.

"Do you have any idea what you set off in there?" he continues, stepping closer. "The press is already tearing it apart. You didn't just speak for yourself, you turned his absence into a public verdict."

"I didn't make his absence a public verdict," Isla snaps. "He did. All I wanted was for people to be honest about him."

His gaze searches her face, as if he's looking for something to grab onto. "Honest would've been waiting."

"Waiting for what?" she demands. "For someone to give me permission to exist in the story of my own father? I've waited twenty-four years. How much longer do I need to wait?"

Silence crackled between them.

She feels eyes on them, glances quickly averted, conversations lowering in pitch. Their tension has weight. Gravity. And people are beginning to notice.

"Not here," he says tightly. "If you're going to do this, don't do it in front of an audience. You've already done that once today."

Isla's mouth curves into something sharp. "Funny. That didn't seem to bother you when the audience was worshipping him."

His jaw flexes. "Come on."

She should refuse.

She doesn't, because it feels good to get out this brewing anger.

They move down a side corridor into a smaller sitting room that smells faintly of leather and old books. The door closes behind them with a soft, final click.

The silence is immediate.

He turns to face her, anger coiled beneath restraint. "You don't get to rewrite his life because you're angry."

Isla laughs, short and incredulous. "Rewrite? I barely wrote a footnote."

"You stood up in front of hundreds of people and reduced him to his worst failure."

"And you've been doing the opposite," she fires back. "Turning him into a saint."

"That's not fair."

"No?" Isla steps closer, exhaustion stripping away her caution. "Then tell me, where was he on my tenth birthday? Or my fifteenth? Or the day I won my first international competition?"

He doesn't answer.

She presses on, voice sharpening. "Where was he when I was practicing six hours a day? When I was throwing up from nerves before performances? When I was crying alone in hotel rooms because my mother was too busy managing my career to notice I wanted my father?"

"He sent money," he says quietly.

The words are cold and mocking.

Isla stiffens. "Money. Oh yeah, that's right, money eases a child's pain when other kids have fathers and know that she doesn't. Money gives them a hug and tells them to sleep well tonight."

"That's not what I meant."

"That's exactly what you meant," she says. "Because that's the version of him you're defending. The one who thought wiring money absolved him of everything else."

His jaw tightens. "You don't know him."

The words cut deeper than she expected.

"You're right," Isla says sharply. "I don't. And that's my point."

She takes a breath. "So who are you, exactly? You keep acting like you own him."

He hesitates.

Then he straightens, like he's made a decision.

"My name is Callum Fraser," he says. "And he raised me."

The word *raised me*, lands like a gut punch. Did her father have an illegitimate son that she knew nothing about? He could raise Callum Fraser, but refused to see her?

Something twisted painfully in her chest.

"He rescued me," Callum continues, voice rough. "He and my father were bandmates. Keir gave me a home when no one else would."

Her anger flares, hot and immediate. "So he had room in his life for you, just not his daughter."

Callum flinches. "It wasn't like that."

"Wasn't it?" she demands. "Because it sounds exactly like that."

She hates the jealousy burning through her. Hates that she wants to scream at him for existing in a space she was never allowed into.

"You got the version of him I never did," she says. "The one who showed up."

Callum's voice drops. "You think it was perfect?"

"I think it was *something*," Isla says. "Which is more than I got."

Silence stretches.

Callum runs a hand through his hair. "He wasn't easy."

"I'm sure."

"He was complicated. Selfish. Brilliant. Exhausting."

"I'm sure," she repeats, bitter. "But he chose you. Not me."

Callum looks at her, really looks, and something shifts in his expression.

"He chose you, too," he says quietly.

Isla laughs, the sound breaking. "No. He didn't."

"He sent money. He kept tabs—"

"He stayed away," she cuts in. "And that was a choice."

They stand there, grief crackling between them, attraction humming beneath it in a way she hates.

She hates that he smells like soap, smoke, and something grounding.

She hates that he knows things about her father she will never know.

"Why does this bother you so much?" Isla asks suddenly. "Why does my truth threaten you?"

Callum's jaw tightens. "Because I loved him. I wasn't his biological son, but he took care of me and raised me like his own after my father was killed in a plane crash."

The admission hits hard.

"So did I," Isla says softly. "I envisioned him coming to one of my concerts. I had dreams that someday we would reunite, and he would ask for my forgiveness. And now, those dreams are just dust in the wind."

Her chest aches with unshed tears. Tears for the dreams that would never be realized.

Callum looks away first.

For a moment, the anger drains out of the room, leaving only rawness behind.

"You didn't fake it," he says finally.

"I'm proud of that," Isla replies.

"You shouldn't be."

"Why?" she challenges. "Because it makes you uncomfortable?"

"Because it hurts," he says.

"So does pretending."

Footsteps echo in the corridor outside, pulling them back toward reality.

Callum steps away, creating distance that feels like loss. "This isn't over," he says quietly.

"No," Isla agrees. "It isn't. Anytime you want to spar, let me know. I'm up for the challenge."

They leave separately.

Back in the gallery, the party continues as if nothing has shifted. Laughter. Glasses clinking. Lives moving on.

Isla catches her reflection again, eyes bright, cheeks flushed, alive with emotion.

She presses a hand briefly to her chest.

She didn't fake grief.

She told the truth.

And in doing so, she collided headfirst with the one man in this castle who loved her father enough to hate her for it.

Which somehow feels like the beginning of something far more dangerous than either of them is ready for.

CHAPTER 6

The castle does not mourn.

It endures.

That is Callum Fraser's first thought when gray morning light seeps through the narrow windows and spills across stone floors that have known centuries of footsteps. He has been awake for hours, pacing corridors that still feel like Keir might step out of any doorway and tell him to stop wearing a path in the rugs.

The house is too quiet.

Not empty, never empty, but hollowed, like a chest after something vital has been cut out. Keir's absence is everywhere. In the silence where music should be. In the cold hearth. In the way the walls seem to be watching him, waiting to see what he'll do next.

Callum stands in the library with a mug of coffee gone untouched in his hand, staring out at the beauty of the land. Fog clings to the land, lifting slowly, revealing fields dark with damp and stubborn with life. This place has survived wars, betrayals, and entire bloodlines rising and falling.

It should survive this.

But survival isn't the same as belonging.

Keir had taken him in when no one else wanted him. Had pulled him out of a school that smelled like bleach and quiet cruelty, signed papers without hesitation, and driven him here without asking whether Callum deserved it or even wanted to live here.

You stay, you follow my rules. You don't want to obey; you can leave.

Callum had stayed.

He had learned structure. Discipline. Responsibility. He had learned how to stand still when anger threatened to consume him. How to build something instead of burn it down.

And Keir, brilliant, selfish, impossible Keir, had promised him this place.

Not in a will. Not in ink.

But in late-night conversations. In shared silences. In the way Keir spoke about the castle like a living thing they were both responsible for.

This place is yours someday, boy. Don't let it rot.

Callum had believed him.

The library door opens.

Belief becomes fragile.

Andrew Bell enters first, carrying a thick leather folder that looks far too heavy for the damage it contains. His expression is composed, professional, almost kind, the face of a man who knows this will hurt and intends to deliver the pain efficiently.

Behind him comes Isla MacLaren and her mother.

Callum turns.

Isla looks different in daylight. Less volatile than she did at the funeral, but sharper for it. She wears dark trousers and a fitted jacket, her auburn hair pulled back tight, her face closed off like a door with the lock thrown. She looks like someone who has already decided not to stay.

Her mother, Alisa, is another thing entirely.

Alisa MacLaren's gaze sweeps the room with practiced

appraisal, the shelves of rare books, the antique desk, the carved fireplace. She is not looking at memories. She is looking at assets.

Callum recognizes fear when he sees it.

Not grief.

Fear.

Fear of losing the monthly checks that have cushioned her life for decades. Fear of watching the last tie to Keir's money snap and leave her exposed.

They take their seats at the long table.

Callum sits opposite Isla, tension coiling low and tight in his chest. He hasn't spoken to her since the night of the funeral reception. He hasn't stopped thinking about her, either, which irritates him more than anything else.

All that auburn hair, that stubborn tilt of her chin, and those full lips that are inviting. What would she taste like?

Bell clears his throat.

"Thank you for meeting this morning," he says. "I'll proceed."

Proceed, Callum thinks. *Get it over.*

Like this is orderly. Like this isn't a reckoning.

"This is the last will and testament of Keir MacLaren," Bell begins, opening the folder. "Executed on March twelfth—"

Callum stops listening to the date.

Dates don't matter.

Promises do.

"The estate includes multiple properties, intellectual rights, publishing income, performance royalties, and liquid investments—"

Alisa leans forward slightly, fingers tightening together.

Callum keeps his eyes on Bell.

"And," Bell continues, "the primary residence known as MacLaren Castle."

Here it comes.

Callum's pulse spikes.

Bell reads carefully, as if gentleness might blunt the blow.

I leave a quarter of my financial assets to Alisa MacLaren and the rest to my daughter, Isla MacLaren. I leave my primary residence, including all attached lands, fixtures, and contents, to my daughter, Isla MacLaren, to do with as she sees fit.

The words land like a physical strike.

Callum doesn't breathe.

This includes the right to retain, occupy, lease, or sell said property at her sole discretion.

Sell.

The word detonates.

"That's wrong," Callum says flatly.

Bell looks up. "I'm afraid it isn't."

"He told me this place would be mine," Callum snaps. "He promised—"

"Verbal assurances," Bell interrupts gently, "do not supersede a valid will."

Callum grips the edge of the table, knuckles whitening.

Across from him, Isla says nothing.

That silence feels deliberate. Strategic.

"So that's it?" Callum demands, turning to her. "You've been here two days, and you're going to sell the only home I've ever known?"

"Yes," Isla says.

One word.

Clean. Cold. Final.

Alisa exhales, relief slipping through before she can hide it. "We'll need to discuss valuation and timeline, of course."

Callum's vision narrows.

"You've never been here," he says to Isla, voice rough. "You don't know this place. You don't know what it means."

"And I don't want to," Isla replies. "It isn't mine."

"It kept me alive," Callum says. "It gave me structure. A future."

"That doesn't make it yours," she counters.

"It makes it earned," he snaps.

Alisa scoffs. "Keir made his intentions clear."

"No," Callum says, turning on her. "He didn't. He never changed the will."

Bell nods. "That is correct."

Callum whips back. "Why?"

Bell hesitates, then sighs. "Keir was… conflicted."

Conflicted.

The word feels like betrayal.

Keir had years. Decades. He had time to fix this, and he didn't.

"Am I mentioned?" Callum asks, already bracing himself.

Bell flips a page.

I leave Callum Fraser a lifetime right of residence within the castle, subject to legal review, along with a trust sufficient for his maintenance.

A leash.

Permission to stay, not ownership.

Alisa's mouth tightens. "That complicates matters."

"It ensures Mr. Fraser isn't displaced," Bell replies.

Isla's eyes flicker, surprise, irritation, something else she quickly smothers. "So I can't sell."

"Not immediately," Bell says. "The will mandates a review period."

"How long?" Isla demands.

"Ninety days minimum."

The silence that follows is heavy and electric.

Callum feels something cold settle into his bones.

They're trapped.

Together.

"That's unacceptable," Isla snaps.

"It's binding," Bell replies calmly.

Alisa stiffens. "We have obligations."

"You'll have to manage them," Bell says. "Miss MacLaren must remain on the premises during the review. For ninety days, she cannot leave."

Isla turns sharply toward Callum. "You planned this."

He lets out a harsh laugh. "You think I wanted this?"

"You're benefiting."

"No," he says. "I'm surviving."

Bell closes the folder. "I'll return tomorrow with the next steps. I advise restraint."

Restraint.

The solicitor leaves.

The door closes behind him with a sound that feels final.

Silence floods the room.

Isla pushes back her chair. "I'm selling this place the moment I legally can."

Callum stands too. "Not without a fight."

Her lips curve, sharp and defiant. "Good."

The challenge hangs between them.

"You hate him," Callum says suddenly.

Isla turns back. "I hate what he didn't give me."

"He saved my life," Callum says, the words ripping out of him before he can stop them. "He pulled me out of hell. He was present. Patient. Protective."

"And absent from mine," Isla fires back. "Your version of him doesn't erase that."

"Your anger feels personal," Callum admits. "Like you're attacking the man who raised me."

"That's because he didn't raise *me*," Isla snaps. "And I'm done pretending that doesn't matter."

They stand there, grief and fury tangling, attraction simmering beneath it in a way neither of them wants.

Callum realizes, with bone-deep certainty, that this is no longer just about property.

It's about loyalty.

Belonging.

Who gets to claim a man when he's gone?

If Isla wants war, he will give it to her.

He will not lose the castle.

He will not lose Keir.

And he will not lose himself, even if despising Isla becomes the hardest thing he's ever had to do. Because all that auburn hair and those expressive emerald eyes are like a calling card, tempting him. Damn, he'd like to kiss her.

CHAPTER 7

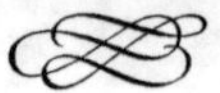

*I*sla MacLaren has always known when a conversation is about to turn ugly.

It begins as a tightening behind her ribs, a shallow breath that refuses to go all the way in. Her mother's tone shifts, barely, almost imperceptibly, but Isla hears it the way she hears a wrong note in a chord. The warmth drains out. The performance ends. What remains is sharpened, precise, and determined to win.

They are in a sitting room off the main corridor, one of those castle rooms that feels ceremonial rather than lived in. The ceilings are too high. The furniture is too heavy. The air smells faintly of stone and polish, like history scrubbed clean and presented for inspection.

A tray of tea rests untouched on a low table between two sofas. Steam curls upward in delicate threads, as if the castle itself is trying to pretend they're here for something civilized.

Isla sits on the edge of the sofa, spine straight, hands folded loosely in her lap. Her posture is flawless. Years of lessons have trained her body to behave even when her emotions threaten revolt. Calm has always been her armor.

And yet she knows her mother is furious at her choice.

58

Alisa paces.

Back and forth across the thick rug, heels clicking softly. She hasn't sat since they arrived. She hasn't touched the tea. Her movements are clipped, restless, controlled, like a woman circling a problem she intends to crush.

"This is reckless," her mother says. "Absolutely reckless."

Isla waits a beat before answering. She's learned that timing matters. A response delivered too quickly sounds emotional. Too slowly, and it sounds weak.

"I'm staying," Isla says, determination layering beneath the two words.

Alisa stops short. Turns. Her eyes narrow.

"No, you're not."

Isla lifts her gaze. "The will requires ninety days."

The words land harder than she expects.

Alisa's mouth tightens. "The will," she snaps, like the phrase itself offends her, "is not worth destroying your career over. Let that kilt man have the castle. Who cares?"

"I'm not destroying anything."

"You have a concert in New York in six weeks," Alisa fires back instantly. "Then Boston. Then Paris. Contracts you signed. Venues that don't reschedule because someone wants to play heiress in a castle."

Isla rises slowly. Her legs feel steady, grounded in a way she doesn't expect. "I can practice here. Fly to the city for one night and then return. I won't miss any concert dates."

Alisa lets out a short, sharp laugh. "Practice isn't the problem. Perception is."

She steps closer, lowering her voice as if the walls themselves might be listening.

"Do you have any idea how fast this turns into a circus?" Alisa continues. "Biographers. Documentarians. Lawyers. Everyone with a grudge or a theory crawling out of the wood-work. Someone claiming they were promised this place.

Someone claiming they were promised *him*. Or worse, someone claiming they were promised you. I've lived in the circus; you never have."

Isla's jaw tightens as understanding dawns. "This isn't about missing a concert."

"It is absolutely about that," Alisa snaps. "Everything you have depends on discipline. On control. On consistency. Classical music does not forgive instability."

"Neither do you," Isla says quietly.

Alisa recoils slightly, then schools her expression. "I have spent your entire life protecting you from your father's circus."

"You've been managing me," Isla says. "There's a difference."

Alisa exhales sharply. "You were a child."

"I'm not anymore."

Alisa's eyes flash. "Then stop acting like one."

The words sting more than Isla expects. And she suddenly wonders when the last time she defied her mother was. When has she ever been truly independent? But it's more than that. It's the fact that she's staying in her father's castle. The man her mother hated.

Alisa's mouth hardens. "The man who nearly ruined us."

"I was a baby. You mean the man who nearly ruined you. The man who paid for my entire life," Isla counters.

The silence between them cracks like ice.

"He paid because it was easier than showing up," Alisa says. "He paid so he wouldn't have to explain himself. So he wouldn't have to change."

"And you let him," Isla says. "You took the money every month."

Could her mother have prevented her from ever seeing her father? The thought sneaks into her brain like a worm, creating chaos.

"I took it because it was owed," Alisa snaps. "Because he didn't get to walk away without consequences."

"And while you were taking it," Isla says slowly, "you were deciding everything else."

Alisa stiffens. "I made sure you succeeded."

"Did I?" Isla asks.

The question hangs there.

Alisa's gaze flickers, just for a second.

And Isla feels something shift.

"You chose my teachers," Isla continues. "My repertoire. Which competitions I entered. Which interviews I gave. You've done it all, Mother."

"That's called guidance."

"You chose when I rested. When I pushed. When I smiled."

Alisa folds her arms. "You needed structure."

"You chose my agent," Isla says.

Alisa's lips press into a thin line.

"You chose which offers I saw," Isla presses.

"That's not—"

"Did you ever show me the Berlin offer?" Isla asks.

The words slip out before she can stop them.

Alisa freezes.

The silence is absolute.

Isla's heart begins to pound. "There *was* an offer, wasn't there?"

Alisa turns away, pacing again. "Berlin would have been a distraction."

"You said they never called," Isla whispers.

"They weren't right for you."

"You decided that?"

"I knew what was best."

Isla's chest tightens painfully. "What about Vienna?"

"That schedule was too aggressive."

"What about the London masterclass?"

"You were exhausted."

"I wasn't exhausted," Isla says. "I was twenty."

Alisa whirls back toward her. "And you were fragile."

The words are a lie and twisted to her mother's advantage.

"I was talented," Isla says. "And ambitious. And scared, but not fragile."

Alisa's voice sharpens. "You were my responsibility."

"I was your project."

Alisa flinches.

The truth lands with brutal clarity.

"You organized my career," Isla says, her voice steady even as her hands begin to shake. "You filtered the world, so I only saw what you wanted me to see. Did you also keep him from me?"

Her mother gasped, her eyes darting nervously around the room, like Keir would walk in and announce the truth. "Never. He could have seen you any time. I protected you from chaos."

Something in her body seemed to tense.

"You protected yourself," Isla says. "And now you're afraid I'll learn the truth and you'll lose control."

Alisa stares at her, breathing hard. "There is only one truth. He never wanted to be a father. He didn't want to see you. Don't buy into their lies. This place will destroy your control. Your career."

"That's why you want me gone."

Alisa doesn't deny it.

"This castle isn't just about him," Isla continues. "It's about what happens when I'm not under your thumb."

"That's not fair."

"It's accurate."

Alisa's voice drops. "You don't understand how easily this can all disappear."

Isla laughs softly. "You mean my career?"

"Yes."

"No," Isla says. "You mean *yours*."

The accusation lands clean and final.

Alisa straightens, smoothing her expression like she's facing an investor instead of her daughter. "You do not belong here," she says. "This castle will rewrite things that don't need rewriting."

Why did her mother appear to be nervous?

"I need the truth."

"You need to get on a plane," Alisa snaps. "You can grieve from New York."

Isla shakes her head. "Who says I'm grieving? You're afraid."

"Yes," Alisa says fiercely. "I am afraid of watching you throw away everything I sacrificed for a man who couldn't stay sober or faithful long enough to raise his own child."

"I'm not staying for him."

"Then why?"

Isla meets her mother's gaze, unwavering. "Because I want to learn about my sperm donor. Not to honor him, but to understand where I come from. And for the first time in my life, I want to make a choice you didn't approve."

Alisa stares at her. "You are choosing him over me."

The accusation slices deep.

"I'm choosing myself," Isla says. "I want to learn about my genes. I want to make certain that the description of my father that you gave me agrees with others who knew him. I need to know the truth."

Alisa turns toward the door, anger brittle and sharp. "Fine. Stay. But when this costs you your career, don't expect me to save you."

"I won't."

Alisa pauses, hand on the knob. "Ninety days," she says. "Then you come home."

"Ninety days," Isla said, not willing to promise her mother that she'd return.

The door closes with a loud, angry boom. The kind of sound of someone leaving, angry, frustrated, and filled with rage.

For the first time in her adult life, Isla has not agreed with her mother, and it feels strangely freeing.

The castle does not react.

No thunder. No collapse. No sudden rush of people.

Just silence.

Isla stands there, heart racing, the weight of what she's learned pressing down on her.

She sinks back onto the sofa as if her legs have finally given up pretending. The tea tray sits untouched, steam thinning, cups still perfectly aligned. A small, irrational part of her wants to sweep it onto the floor and listen to porcelain shatter against stone, proof she can break something in this place that broke her first.

Instead, she presses her fingers to her sternum and breathes.

Alone.

The word lands harder now that it's real.

She closes her eyes and sees the funeral again, not the casket, not the faces, but the piano. The weight of the bench beneath her. The way her hands didn't tremble. The way her voice stayed steady as she sang.

He loved music. He just didn't love being a father.

The chapel had gasped. Isla hadn't looked up. She hadn't needed to.

Honesty had carried her through.

Here, honesty feels heavier. Like a weight bearing down.

She stands, because sitting still will swallow her whole, and steps into the corridor. Her footsteps echo, following her like a reminder that she exists here now, whether she wants to or not.

The castle unfolds around her, stone and shadow, history layered thick as dust. Portraits line the walls: stern men, sharp-eyed women, ancestors who look like they would never apologize for wanting more. She wonders which of them Keir resembled. She wonders if anyone in this bloodline ever learned how to stay.

A study door stands ajar. She pauses, peering inside. A desk cluttered with papers. Sheet music stacked carelessly. Coffee rings on polished wood. Evidence of a life lived without clean edges.

She doesn't touch anything.

Not yet. She isn't ready to dig into her father's secrets, but knows sometime during these ninety days, she will search to find out what kind of man he really was. If he was the vile creature her mother painted him or if he was just a man.

Farther on, a room filled with records and books about composition, guitar technique, theory. Framed photos, Keir on stage, Keir laughing with bandmates, Keir alive in a way Isla recognizes with a painful jolt.

She turns away before the jealousy can root itself. They knew him, she didn't.

The staircase beneath her hand is worn smooth, the stone cool and solid. *Hell has excellent stonework*, she thinks, and the humorless thought keeps her moving.

At the end of a quieter corridor, she stops.

The music room.

She opens the door.

The piano sits at the center like an altar, glossy black, patient, waiting.

Isla approaches slowly. Rests her hand on the lid. The surface is cool beneath her palm.

She sits.

Adjusts the bench. Finds the pedals.

For a moment, nothing happens.

Then she presses a single key.

The note rings out, pure and unafraid.

Another. Then another.

The melody forms hesitantly, exploratory, as if feeling its way through unfamiliar territory. Isla lets it wander. Lets it stumble. Lets dissonance exist without apology.

She plays angry first. Sharp-edged and relentless. Emptying

her soul of the dire emotion onto the keys of the piano, in the music she's creating.

Then sorrow underneath it.

Then something quieter. Curious.

She doesn't realize she's humming until she hears herself.

Not words. Just breath on pitch.

Tears slip silently down her cheeks, but her hands don't falter.

She plays until her wrists ache.

Until the music resolves into something steady and determined.

The final chord lingers.

Silence settles, not hollow this time, but alive.

Isla lifts her hands from the keys.

She is not alone.

She doesn't turn. Doesn't need to.

Let them hear, she thinks. Let them feel her emotions and absorb her pain.

She sets her fingers back on the keys, not to perform, not to impress, but to claim the one thing in this castle that is hers.

And she begins to play again.

CHAPTER 8

Callum knows better than to linger outside the music room.

He tells himself that as he stands in the corridor, one hand braced against the cold stone wall, the sound of the piano spilling through the thick oak door like a confession he was never meant to hear.

He should leave.

That's the rule he's lived by his entire adult life, knowing when to step back, knowing when something isn't yours to touch. Keir taught him that much, if nothing else. Some things belonged to the music. Some things belonged to the moment. And some things, no matter how badly you wanted them, were never meant to be claimed.

But Callum doesn't move.

Not the polished, pristine kind of playing he's heard at galas and fundraisers. Not the flawless execution meant to impress donors and critics. This is something else entirely, raw and unguarded, the sound of someone bleeding through their hands and daring the room to hold it.

The first notes are tentative. Searching.

Then they deepen.

The melody stumbles, recovers, fractures again. Dissonance creeps in, sharp and unapologetic, and Callum's chest tightens because he recognizes that sound. It's the sound of someone refusing to smooth the edges of their pain for anyone else's comfort.

He closes his eyes.

He has heard Keir play like this.

Not in public. Never in front of an audience. Only late at night, when the house was quiet, and the whisky was untouched because Keir needed his hands steady. That was when the music came out like this, angry, broken, demanding to be heard.

But Keir's daughter commanded the piano like a captain commanding a ship.

Callum swallowed hard.

Damn her.

Damn her for sounding like him. Damn her for being so good that he's drawn inside her pain.

The door creaks faintly as Callum slips inside the room, but Isla doesn't stop. She doesn't even falter. The music swells, growing more confident, more insistent, as if she's decided something mid-phrase and refuses to let go of it.

Callum presses his palm flat against the wall.

This is the woman who will take the castle from him. He's drawn to her, and the realization burns, sharp and infuriating.

The thought lands heavy and bitter.

Ninety days.

That's what the solicitor said, reading the will in a voice so neutral, it felt like an insult. Ninety days for Isla MacLaren to live here, to breathe the air, to let the place work its way into her bones. Ninety days before everything Callum has protected, repaired, and held together with his bare hands could be gone.

And yet—

He listens.

And something inside him fractures anyway.

The piano shifts into a new movement. The anger doesn't disappear, but it changes shape. Becomes something steadier. Purposeful. Like a vow set to rhythm.

Callum's throat tightens.

Earlier, without her knowledge, he'd seen her, standing in the sitting room, spine straight, chin lifted, defiance simmering just beneath the surface. He'd known then that whatever battle she'd just fought with her mother hadn't ended cleanly. He'd seen it in her eyes. The way control had been ripped away and replaced with something sharper.

Freedom.

The music reflects it now.

She's not playing for applause. She's not playing for legacy. She's playing like someone reclaiming a part of themselves that was never meant to be borrowed, cultivated, or approved.

Callum exhales slowly. The music reminds him of how he felt the day he left the boys' school: raw, unmoored, and carrying freedom that felt too much like betrayal. How the castle had welcomed him with open arms and memories of his father.

This castle was never just stone and mortar to him. It was survival. It was proof that someone wanted him when no one else did. Keir had dragged him out of a hell Callum barely talks about anymore, out of the school, out of the fights, out of the spiral he'd been headed toward.

"This place is yours," Keir had said once, slurring slightly, hand heavy on Callum's shoulder. "One day."

Not written. Not promised in ink.

But meant.

And now Isla sits at the piano like she was born to it, like she belongs here in a way Callum never quite allowed himself to believe he did.

The music softens.

Callum opens his eyes.

Inside the music room, the door is still closed. He could turn away. Walk out and down the corridor. Pretend he never heard this moment.

He doesn't.

Because the next notes aren't just beautiful.

They're devastating.

They carry loss, not Keir's, not even Isla's, but something deeper. The grief of a child who waited too long for someone who never came. The quiet, aching loneliness of hotel rooms and rehearsals and applause that never quite filled the hollow.

Callum feels it settle in his chest like a weight.

He remembers Isla at the funeral, sitting rigid and composed, voice steady as she sang words that cut clean through the chapel. He remembers thinking she was made of steel.

He was wrong.

She's made of fire and fracture and something that refuses to break cleanly.

The music crescendos, hands moving faster now, confidence replacing hesitation. The melody doesn't resolve neatly. It refuses closure. It demands space.

Callum's fingers curl into a fist.

How is he supposed to hate her?

Callum knows that with brutal clarity.

Wanting her is a liability. And yet it's all he can do to keep from rushing over to the piano and pulling her into his arms and whispering he feels it too.

Desire makes men careless. Soft. It makes them hesitate when they should stand firm. He's seen it destroy livelihoods, families, and entire legacies. Keir himself had been proof of that.

And yet—

Isla sits at the piano like she belongs to the room, like the castle shaped itself around her sound. Like she could dismantle everything Callum has protected simply by staying.

If he lets himself want her, he won't fight hard enough.

If he doesn't fight hard enough, he loses the castle.

And if he loses the castle—

He loses the last place he was ever chosen. The last place to accept him.

How is he supposed to protect the castle from a woman who sounds like she understands its soul better than anyone alive?

The final chord rings out, vibrating through the stone, lingering in the air like a held breath.

Silence follows.

Callum waits for her to stand. To move. To acknowledge his presence.

She doesn't.

Instead, she sets her fingers back on the keys.

Not to perform.

Not to impress.

But to claim the moment.

Callum pushes off the wall before he can talk himself out of it.

Isla doesn't turn.

Her shoulders are squared, posture perfect even in stillness. A tear slips down her cheek, catching the light before she wipes it away with the back of her hand like she refuses to apologize for it.

"You play with emotion," Callum says quietly.

She freezes.

For a moment, he thinks she might tell him to leave. He half-expects it. He deserves it.

Instead, she exhales slowly.

"I didn't know anyone was listening."

"I was trying not to," he admits.

That earns him a glance.

Her eyes are red-rimmed but fierce, alive with something he doesn't have a name for. Not grief. Not anger.

Ownership.

"This room carries sound," she says. "The sound wants to be heard."

Odd how much father and daughter are alike.

Callum nods. "Keir used to say that."

Her fingers still.

"He played here?"

"Every night," Callum says. "When the world got too loud, and he wanted solace."

She looks back at the piano, something unreadable crossing her face.

"He taught me not to interrupt," Callum adds. "Said the music would stop when it was ready."

Isla's mouth curves faintly. "Smart man."

Callum almost laughs.

Smart wasn't the word he'd use. More like driven, haunted, and more talented than any musician he'd ever met. Even his own father.

She turns on the bench then, finally facing him fully. "You think I'm here to take something from you."

The directness knocks the breath from him.

"Yes," he says, just as plainly. Knowing she was voicing his biggest fear.

She nods once, as if she expected it. "You think the castle is yours."

"Your father promised it to me. I think I earned it."

"So did I," she says softly. "I want to learn more about my father. Not just what my mother has told me. I need answers and I believe the castle can tell me about my sperm donor."

The memory of his own father, laughing and loving him, rattles Callum. He hates those two words, but understands why she feels that way.

The words hang between them, not hostile, but sharp.

Callum runs a hand through his hair. "You don't know what this place means to me."

The castle has been his home for the last fifteen years. A place of sanctuary. Of acceptance and even love.

She rises with deliberate grace, her blouse tracing her curves, her waist lean and distracting. The instinctive pull to touch her slams into him, and he swallows it like a weakness.

"You don't know what it cost me to get here."

They stare at each other across the piano, an altar, a battleground, a confession neither of them asked for.

Callum feels the truth pressing against his ribs.

"I don't want to fight you," he says, wishing they had met under different circumstances. Why had Keir never told him about his daughter? Even in his drunken state, he'd never mentioned the girl on the other side of the pond. A woman who played the piano like a dream, even better than her father.

Isla's gaze flickers. "Neither do I."

"And yet," Callum continues, "I don't know how to stand by and watch you take the one thing that feels like mine. The place that is my everything."

Her voice is quiet but unyielding. "I don't know how to walk away from the only place that's ever felt honest. A building that holds secrets I need to learn."

Something in Callum shifts.

This isn't about a will.

This isn't even about Keir.

It's about two people standing in the wreckage of the same man, each holding a different piece of what he left behind. One searching for answers and the one wanting to hold onto a peaceful time in his life.

Callum steps back first.

Not in surrender.

In recognition.

"You play like a goddess," he says, before he can stop himself.

Isla blinks, startled.

Then her chin lifts. "And you guard this place like it's alive."

"Because it is," Callum says, "to me."

His heart cracks at the thought of leaving it all behind. The memories, the music. Everything that had brought him back to life after his father's death.

She nods slowly. "Then I guess we're both staying. For now."

The tension snaps taut between them, electric, dangerous, undeniable. Maybe he should say thank you, but it's his home. And that's a bridge too far, even for him.

Callum turns toward the door, desperate to escape the pull of her sensuality, the way her voice and her music wrap around him and refuse to let go.

"Get some rest," he says. "The castle doesn't sleep easily. Let me know when you're ready to begin your search. Maybe I can help."

Or maybe he'd only lead her astray. He hadn't yet decided which path would help him keep the castle.

As he leaves, he knows one thing with absolute certainty.

Losing the castle will break him.

But letting Isla go—

What is it about this woman, her long red hair, her emerald eyes sharp with emotion and fire, eyes too much like Keir's, that makes him wary and wanting in equal measure?

CHAPTER 9

The castle doesn't sleep, but it watches.

Isla feels it the moment she steps into the corridor, the air cool and faintly damp, stone breathing in slow, patient rhythms. Morning light slants through narrow windows, catching dust motes and turning them into drifting constellations. Somewhere deeper in the castle, a door closes. Footsteps echo and fade.

After yesterday, she had spent time in her room, relaxing and trying to decide what she hoped to accomplish while she was here. This morning, she knew and was going to begin her search in earnest, but first, she had to learn the castle.

Didn't she deserve to know if her mother's version of her father was correct? Maybe she could find the divorce papers and see if there was any information about why her father chose never to see her again.

She hasn't seen Callum this morning. That should be a relief.

Instead, it leaves her unsettled, as if something unfinished is humming beneath her skin. The absence sharpens into an edge she hasn't felt in years, not nerves, not fear.

Defiance.

And something more dangerous.

Desire.

It unsettles her that her body noticed him before her mind caught up. That it answered him without permission, without logic. She doesn't understand why it chose *him*, this man who stands in her way, who challenges her footing in a place that already feels unsteady.

Maybe it's because men have always come second in her life.

Because boyfriends were rare, brief, and never quite fitting. Most men lost interest once they realized she belonged to the piano, that hours at the keys weren't a phase but a devotion. That her life was measured in rehearsals and flights, in performances that demanded more than constancy ever could.

She had learned, quietly, not to expect much from them.

And now this man, this infuriating, guarded, impossible man, has awakened something she thought she'd trained herself out of needing.

That realization unsettles her far more than his absence ever could.

She told Callum she would search, and he offered her his help, though she wasn't certain he meant what he said. She told her mother she would search. She told herself that if she stayed in this castle and did nothing but play music and sleep badly, then her mother would still be right, this would all be indulgence. Emotion. Chaos.

Truth requires action and she intends to find that missing puzzle of her life. Her father and why he never visited her.

Isla stops outside a door she recognizes only because she's passed it twice already.

Keir's private study.

Not the conference room near the main hall, the tasteful room lawyers like to gesture toward. This one sits deeper in the castle, down a narrower corridor, its door darker, more worn. The handle is polished smooth from years of use.

Her pulse kicks.

This isn't accidental anymore.

She reaches for the handle.

The door isn't locked.

It opens with a faint protest, hinges whispering like they disapprove.

The room smells different from the rest of the castle, older somehow. Paper and leather and dust layered with something faintly sharp, like old smoke or ink. Light filters through tall windows, illuminating a broad desk scarred with use. Old guitars line the wall. Music is scattered on the desk, and some Diamond record awards line the walls, while others sit waiting to be hung. So much paraphernalia.

This room feels lived in.

Isla moves closer to the desk.

Her fingers brush a stack of loose papers, receipts, handwritten notes, a folded sheet of hotel stationery with a city name scrawled across the top. Glasgow. Berlin. Los Angeles. Lives reduced to ink and impulse.

She lifts a photograph.

Keir stands in the center, arm slung around a group of people she doesn't recognize. Everyone is laughing. Everyone looks alive in a way that has nothing to do with fame and everything to do with belonging.

Isla's throat tightens.

"You look happy," she murmurs, then stiffens at the sound of her own voice in the room.

She shouldn't be here. But she doesn't care. He's her father. He's dead, and she's going to go through his things and hopefully find the answers she needs to her questions.

That thought doesn't stop her from opening a notebook. The handwriting is unmistakable, fast, slanted, and impatient. Lyrics crowd the margins, crossed out and rewritten, emotion spilling wherever it can fit.

One line is underlined so hard, the paper nearly tears.

She deserves better than my silence.

Isla's breath catches.

Her hand trembles as she closes the notebook, heart hammering. This isn't curiosity anymore.

This is intrusion.

She opens a drawer.

Cassette tapes.

Dozens of them, stacked carefully, labeled in Keir's slanted handwriting. Dates. Cities. Some with names she recognizes, bandmates, producers. Others with nothing but a time written beside them.

Her fingers curl around one.

"That's not for you."

Callum's voice cuts through the room like a blade.

Isla spins.

He stands in the doorway, broad shoulders filling the frame, expression closed and unreadable. He hasn't raised his voice. He hasn't moved toward her.

Which makes it worse.

"You said you'd help," Isla says.

His jaw tightens. "I said maybe."

"You followed me."

"I followed the sound of a door that shouldn't have been opened."

Her grip tightens around the tape. "You don't get to decide that."

"This room isn't part of the estate tour."

"Neither is my life," she snaps. "And yet everyone seems comfortable managing it."

He steps into the room, closing the door behind him with deliberate care.

The sound lands heavy.

"You don't know what you're doing," Callum says.

"I know exactly what I'm doing," Isla fires back. "I'm looking for the truth."

His gaze drops to the cassette in her hand.

"That won't give it to you."

"You don't know that."

"I do."

Something sharp flares in his eyes. "Those tapes aren't confessions. They're fragments. Half-thoughts. Bad nights."

"Or honesty," Isla counters.

"Or damage," he says. "You don't listen to a man at his worst and call it truth."

Her pulse pounds. "You did."

He stills.

For a moment, the air between them hums.

"You were there," she presses. "You know things."

"I know enough to tell you to put that down."

Isla lifts her chin. "Make me."

The words fall into the room, reckless and unmistakable.

Callum steps closer.

Not fast. Not angry.

Controlled.

The space between them shrinks to nothing but breath and heat and the faint scent of coffee and wood smoke clinging to his clothes.

"You're trespassing," he says quietly.

"You're hiding things."

"I'm protecting this place. I'm trying to protect your father."

"And I'm trying to understand where I came from."

His gaze drops again, to her hand, to the tape, to the way her fingers are trembling now despite her resolve.

"You think listening to his voice will fix something?" he says. "It won't."

Isla's eyes narrow. "You're not just protecting the castle."

He doesn't answer.

"You're protecting *him*," she presses. "Or at least the version of him you want to preserve."

His jaw flexes. "You don't get to rewrite a man's life from scraps."

"And you don't get to edit it," she shoots back. "You've been deciding what survives him."

That lands.

Callum looks away, just long enough for her to know she's right.

"He trusted me," he says finally.

"To do what?" Isla demands. "Guard the truth? Or bury it? You didn't even know about me."

His gaze snaps back to hers, raw and furious. "To protect what mattered."

"So I didn't matter." The words are ripped from her throat.

Silence stretches, thick and volatile.

Callum steps closer, voice low. "You don't understand the damage this could do."

Isla doesn't retreat. "To whom? My father or me?"

He doesn't answer.

"I understand exactly what you're afraid of."

His breath ghosts her skin. "Do you?"

"Yes," she says. "Losing control."

Something shifts.

Callum's hand lifts.

He doesn't touch her, not yet, but it hovers near her waist, fingers flexing like they're remembering something they shouldn't.

The air goes thin.

Isla's breath catches. She can feel the pull, undeniable and reckless, like standing at the edge of something with no railing.

She tilts her head, just slightly.

Callum swears under his breath.

For one suspended, dangerous second, he doesn't stop himself.

His hand lands on her waist.

Heat explodes through her.

Isla gasps.

His thumb presses in, firm, possessive, like he's forgotten every reason not to. She feels it everywhere, her spine, her knees, the sudden, dizzy awareness of how close his mouth is.

Too close. His full lips are beckoning her, and she wants to know how he tastes.

Her fingers curl into his shirt.

Their foreheads almost touch.

Time fractures.

Isla becomes acutely aware of everything at once: his grip at her waist, the hard line of his body inches from hers, the sound of his breath breaking control. Her pulse stutters, loud enough she's sure he can feel it.

She shouldn't lean in.

She does anyway.

Callum's hand tightens, fingers digging in like he's bracing himself against a fall. His head dips, just enough that she feels the promise of his mouth, the threat of it.

This isn't curiosity.

This is collision.

For one suspended heartbeat, she knows, knows with absolute certainty, that if he kisses her, nothing in this castle will remain intact.

Not the search.

Not the boundaries.

Not either of them.

This is not slow.

This is not careful.

This is the kind of kiss that ruins things.

Callum leans in—

And stops.

The moment shatters.

He drops his hand like it burned him and steps back hard enough to knock into the desk.

"Jesus," he mutters.

Isla's pulse roars in her ears. Her skin feels too tight, too alive.

She stares at him, breath unsteady. "That—"

"Shouldn't have happened," he says sharply.

"But it almost did."

He looks at her then, studies her, something wild and furious and undone flashing across his face.

"That's the problem," he says. "It almost did."

He reaches past her, plucks the cassette from her hand, and sets it back in the drawer with finality.

"This search," he says, voice rough, "just got dangerous."

And before she can answer, before she can think, he turns and leaves the room.

The door slams behind him.

Isla stands there, heart racing, skin still burning where his hand had been.

The castle exhales.

And nothing will ever be simple again.

Isla grabs the cassette and storms toward her room, desire and fury tangling in her blood. She's going to hear his voice. She's going to know the truth. And not even the near kiss, hot, unfinished, and haunting, will derail her.

CHAPTER 10

The next day, Callum avoided the east wing all morning. It was deliberate. Calculated. He gives himself reasons that sound responsible, inventory work, a call he needs to make, a leaking window in the north tower that won't fix itself, but the truth is simpler and harder to face.

He doesn't trust himself around her.

Not after the Keir's private music room.

Not after the heat and the loss of control and the way his hand had known exactly where to go, as if his body had already made decisions his mind hadn't sanctioned. And the touch of her was like a heat he'd never experienced.

So he stays busy. He stays grounded. He keeps to stone and wood and practical things that don't look back at him with eyes full of challenge and fervor and something far more dangerous.

Guilt.

He tells himself Isla MacLaren will be doing what she always does, playing, searching, digging where she shouldn't. He tells himself that if he stays away long enough, the edge will dull. The castle will settle. She will settle.

None of it works.

He hears the piano just after noon.

The sound threads through the stone corridors softly at first, barely there, the way fog rolls in without announcing itself. One note, then another. No flourish. No opening declaration. Just sound, hesitant, spare, almost reluctant.

Callum stops where he is, fingers still on the latch of a supply closet, his breath caught halfway in.

This isn't the music from the night before.

That had been defiant. Angry. A woman staking her claim with both hands and daring the world to argue.

This—

This is something else entirely.

It doesn't build the way a performance does. There's no arc meant for an audience, no clean progression, no satisfying resolution. Notes drift, collide, break apart. Silence stretches too long between phrases, as if she's forgetting to breathe.

Callum's chest tightens.

This isn't technique.

This is grief.

Not the public kind, the kind she'd worn at the funeral with her spine straight and her voice steady. This is private. Unfiltered. A sound made when no one is meant to hear.

And yet—

Here he is. Longing to be near her. Longing to make certain she's all right.

He tells himself he's only passing through. Only checking that the staff have kept the wing secure. Only making sure she isn't doing something that will get her hurt.

It's a lie he doesn't bother to believe.

A chord lands wrong, dissonant and sharp enough that Callum winces.

She doesn't correct it.

She stays there, fingers pressing down as if daring the sound to exist.

Keir used to do that. It drove him crazy, but it was the man's way of expressing his discontent.

Late at night, when the world stopped asking him to be charming, those nights, the music didn't swagger. It wandered. It faltered. It circled wounds Keir never named aloud.

Callum stands in the corridor outside the music room and lets the sound sink into him, cold and unavoidable.

Once again, knowing he shouldn't go in, but unable to stop himself, Callum slips inside the room. Like the great pianist she is, she's practicing.

He counts the beats the way Keir taught him, one, two, three, four, trying to turn music into math, emotion into something manageable. It doesn't work. The rhythm keeps changing, slipping out from under him. Isla isn't counting for anyone. She isn't trying to stay neat.

Her left hand drops into a low, repeating pattern that feels like footsteps on stone. Not running. Not approaching. Just pacing. The right hand answers with a thin, high line that sounds like a voice calling into a room that won't answer back.

Callum feels it in his teeth.

The music isn't pretty. It isn't meant to be. It is brutally honest in a way that makes him want to look away.

He remembers Keir once saying, "If it sounds too beautiful, you're lying." Then Keir had laughed like it was a joke, but he'd played the next chord hard enough to make the keys protest.

Isla plays like she has the same rule carved into her bones.

A pause opens, wide and dangerous, and Callum thinks she's done. Then she comes back with a phrase so simple it almost hurts: three notes, repeated, each time slightly altered, as if she's changing the question because the answer refuses to appear.

Here, there had been this castle, this music room, and a man who played like he was trying to outrun his own ghosts. Now the ghost he was trying to outrun sat at the piano, expressing her emotions in ways her father would have applauded.

The man who came for him is the same man who never came for Isla.

It doesn't make sense.

The music shifts again, and Callum's chest tightens with sudden, unfair anger at Keir, at Isla, at himself. Because the sound proves something Callum doesn't want to admit: Isla didn't inherit money. She inherited the part of Keir that hurts.

How does a man leave this?

How does a father walk away from a child capable of this kind of truth and never look back? Never sit in the back of a hall and listen. Never stand in a doorway and let her playing wreck him.

That isn't the man Callum knew.

Keir was many things: reckless, selfish, addicted to chaos, but he wasn't indifferent. Indifference made him cruel. It made him restless. It made him drink.

So why?

The question digs in deep, sharp as a splinter.

Callum takes one step inside the music room, then stops. If he doesn't stop, he'll do something stupid.

He'll say something that can't be unsaid.

He'll touch her again.

He'll forget she's here to take the castle from him.

The music shifts, lower now, stripped down to a handful of notes, spaced wide. It sounds like waiting. Like standing at a door that never opens and telling yourself you're not waiting at all.

Callum's jaw tightens.

He doesn't announce himself. Doesn't clear his throat. He listens until it hurts.

Isla sits at the piano, posture imperfect for once, shoulders tense, head bowed slightly as if the instrument itself is too heavy. Her bright red hair is pulled back hastily, strands escaping near her neck. She's not dressed for an audience. She's dressed to survive the day.

Her hands move slower than he's seen them before, deliberate, careful, like every note costs something.

The melody turns into something spare and jagged. No prettiness. No comfort. Just the sound of a wound being pressed until it admits it exists.

Callum swallows.

He'd thought she was steel.

Now she's the fracture.

The music thins until only single notes remain. In the gap between them, Callum can hear her breath. He can hear the soft scrape of the bench when she shifts. He can hear the castle settling around them.

Then the line resolves, not into peace, but into stubbornness. A decision made through clenched teeth.

Isla's shoulders lift.

She knows he's there.

Her hands fall from the keys, hovering a moment before lowering to her lap. She sits very still, listening not to the piano but to the room.

"You can stop pretending," she says, voice tight. "I heard you this time."

Callum steps fully into the room.

"I was drawn to the music," he says.

She laughs once, sharp and humorless. "That's what everyone says."

He stays near the door like it's a line he shouldn't cross.

Isla turns on the bench to face him. Her eyes are bright, not with tears, but with the effort of holding them back.

"What do you want?" she asks.

Callum hesitates. The truth feels dangerous.

"The music," he says finally. "It didn't sound like… last night."

"Last night was anger," she snaps. "This is what comes after."

"It sounded like grief," he says.

Her mouth twists. "Congratulations. You're perceptive."

"It didn't feel like performance."

"Because it wasn't."

Silence stretches. The piano sits between them like a witness.

Callum tries for neutral and fails. "Keir taught me everything I know about music."

The words are out before he can stop them.

Isla's expression shatters.

"Of course, he did," she explodes, standing so fast the bench scrapes against the floor. "Why wouldn't he? He gave everything to everyone else. Everyone but me."

Callum stiffens. "That's not—"

"He taught you," she barrels on, voice rising, brittle and sharp. "He taught his bandmates. His friends. His protégés. He poured himself into strangers and called it generosity. But his daughter? Oh fuck, no."

Her hands shake at her sides now, fists clenched. "And then he sent checks and thought that made him decent."

The blow lands hard in Callum's chest. Loyalty flares, hot and automatic.

"That's not the man I knew," he says, too quickly.

Isla laughs, harsh and broken. "Then you didn't know him the way I did."

The second the words leave her mouth, Isla goes still.

Color drains from her face.

"I—" She swallows. "I didn't mean—"

Her hand rises, then drops, useless. Her voice turns small in spite of her. "I'm sorry. That wasn't fair."

"No," Callum agrees. "It wasn't. But I fear it's true."

For a moment, Isla looks like she might bolt, as the room has suddenly become too small to contain her grief. She takes one step, then stops, jaw clenched, forcing herself to stay.

"I don't want to be like this," she says, voice low. "I don't want… you."

It comes out wrong, not what she meant, and her eyes widen with fresh panic.

Callum's pulse kicks. "I know what you mean."

Isla huffs out a breath, then drags a hand through her hair, pulling loose strands tighter as if she can tie her emotions back into place. "I didn't want you to see that," she mutters.

"The anger?" Callum asks.

"No." She gestures between them, then toward her own chest. "The… need. Always the need to know what he thought about my career. About me. About the young woman I've become. And now…nothing."

Callum's throat tightens. He understands need. He's lived with it like a second skin.

"You listened to the tape," he says.

Her eyes flick up, wary. "You knew."

"I guessed."

She nods once, jaw tight. "I did. And it was nothing."

"Nothing?" he repeats.

"Song ideas," she says. "Fragments. Him counting beats, humming melodies, muttering lines. Nothing personal. No confession. No apology. No mention of me."

She tries for a shrug and fails. "It shouldn't have disappointed me. It's exactly what I should have expected."

"But you hoped," Callum says quietly.

Her eyes flash. "I'm not stupid, but yes…I got my hopes up I'd found a message he left me."

"Hoping doesn't make you stupid."

"Don't," she snaps, the word sharp with panic. "Don't be kind."

Callum lets the silence stretch. Kindness is its own kind of danger.

Isla's chin lifts again, defensive. "It was just music," she says, as if repeating it will make it hurt less. "That's all he ever left behind."

Callum's gaze slides to the piano. "Music is never just music."

"That's easy for you to say," she fires back. "You got him."

Callum flinches at the accuracy.

"I got parts of him," he says slowly. "And it wasn't always the good parts."

There were nights, he remembered, taking care of a drunk Keir. A man haunted by ghosts of the past. And now Callum was beginning to understand why.

Isla stills, startled by the admission.

"He could be generous," Callum continues, voice low. "And he could be selfish. Brilliant and cruel in the same hour. He could make you feel chosen and then punish you for believing it."

Isla's throat works. "So why didn't he choose me?"

The question isn't sharp.

It's worse.

It's honest.

Callum has no answer.

He thinks of Keir dragging him out of a future that would have destroyed him. And he thinks of Isla as a child, waiting.

The contradiction doesn't resolve. It only sharpens.

"I don't know," Callum admits. "It makes no sense to me."

The words feel like betrayal and relief.

"But I'm starting to wonder," he adds, "if the man I knew and the man who left you were the same person at all."

Isla stares at him like she can't decide whether she wants to tear the thought apart or cling to it.

"That doesn't make it better," she says.

"No," he agrees. "It makes it complicated."

"Everything about him is," she whispers.

Callum nods. "Keir never did simple."

Isla turns away, palm flattening on the piano as if she needs something solid. "My mother says he didn't want to see me."

Callum's jaw tightens. "Did she say why?"

"She said he chose the music," Isla replies. "That he chose drugs and women and fame. That I was collateral damage."

Callum's mind flashes to Keir sober at three in the morning, staring at nothing like it was a verdict. To the rare nights he wouldn't touch whiskey at all, fingers white around the glass as if refusing himself something.

Callum had assumed it was discipline.

Now he wonders if it was fear.

"What did he say about me?" Isla asks suddenly.

Callum meets her gaze. "He didn't talk about you at all. I learned about you the day he died."

Pain flickers across her face, quick as lightning.

Silence again, thick and breathing.

Callum takes a slow step forward, stopping on the other side of the piano. "I keep asking myself," he says quietly, "how a man can save one kid and abandon another."

Isla's head turns sharply.

Callum holds her gaze. "It doesn't fit."

Her voice comes out thin. "Maybe he recognized that you were in danger and needed rescuing."

Callum nods once. "From a place that would've ruined me."

Jealousy flashes in her eyes, raw, naked, and then regret hits her instantly.

She inhales sharply. "I'm—" She stops, jaw tight. "I'm sorry."

Callum shakes his head. "Don't apologize for wanting what you should've had."

Isla flinches like that's worse than an insult. "Stop."

Callum falls silent.

Isla's hand curls on the piano's edge. "I don't want to be seen like this," she says, voice shaking despite her control. "I don't want you to understand me."

"Why?" Callum asks.

"Because then you'll pity me," she snaps, heat flaring again. "And I refuse to be pitied in my own father's house."

Callum's jaw tightens. "I don't pity you. I just don't understand why Keir did this."

"Everyone looks at me with pity in their eyes. The servants, the press, even you," she shoots back, then closes her eyes, as if the words are a betrayal. She exhales. "God. I'm sorry. I'm just… tired of being the only one who didn't get him."

Callum's chest aches.

Isla opens her eyes again, gaze fierce and guarded. "I listened to the tape because I needed something real," she says. "And all I got was melody."

Callum nods. "That's real."

"It's not enough," she whispers.

"No," Callum agrees.

Callum's gaze catches on the fallboard above the keys. For a moment, he sees a different scene: Keir in this room, palm on that same polished wood, staring at a photograph he kept hidden like a sin. Callum had found it once by accident, a little girl, missing front teeth, grin bright enough to hurt. Keir had snatched it back with a sharpness that felt like fear.

Until this past week, Callum had never known who that child was. Now he realized it was Isla.

Callum almost tells her.

The words rise to his tongue, *He had a photo. He kept of you. Not in the ways that mattered, but—*

He swallows them down.

A photo is not a father. A secret keepsake isn't proof of love. It's proof of something, yes, but Callum doesn't know what, and he won't feed her another half-truth.

Instead, he says, "If there's anything you want to search for, papers, recordings, letters, I can at least tell you where he kept things."

"You're offering to show me where he kept his secrets?" Isla's laugh is thin. "And I'm supposed to trust that you won't hide the parts you don't want me to see?"

Callum's jaw tightens. "We'll discover them together."

Another silence.

Isla drops back onto the bench, not to play, but to sit in the aftermath. Her shoulders rise and fall. "What now?" she asks, voice steadier.

Callum answers honestly. "Now, I don't know."

Isla's laugh is brittle. "Welcome to my life."

Callum watches her fingers hover above the keys. He realizes he's holding his breath again, waiting for the next thing she'll reveal without meaning to.

Instead, she plays one chord, soft, unresolved.

It isn't a performance. It's punctuation.

Callum backs toward the door, slowly. The room feels too tight for both of them.

"I'll give you space," he says.

Isla doesn't look at him. "Thank you," she murmurs, and the words sound like they cost her.

Callum pauses with his hand on the door.

He wants to promise answers. He wants to promise justice. He wants to promise that the castle won't swallow her whole.

Instead, he says, the only honest thing left.

"I don't believe he didn't want you," Callum says quietly.

Isla's head jerks up.

Callum meets her gaze, steady. "I don't know why he stayed away. But I don't believe it was because you weren't worth coming back for."

For one second, Isla looks like she might break.

Then she lifts her chin, the mask snapping back into place.

"Don't," she says, voice low. "Don't give me hope you can't back up."

Callum nods once.

And he leaves the room.

He walks down the corridor with her music clinging to him like smoke, and one thought follows him, relentless and unsettling:

How does a man live with saving one child and walking away from another?

That's not the Keir Callum he knew.

So either Callum never knew him at all—

Or Keir's reason is buried somewhere in this castle, waiting to be found.

And suddenly, he wants to help her find those answers.

CHAPTER 11

*I*sla had had enough. It was time to stop feeling sorry for herself and do something. Walking down the hall, she came to Keir's private study/musical storeroom with intention and determination to learn something.

Not anger. Not grief. Purpose. She's here to learn what he's hiding, and sitting at the piano will just have to wait until this afternoon, after she's exhausted from going through his personal items.

She closed the door behind her and stands still for a moment, palms flat against the wood, letting the room settle around her. The castle hums softly beyond the walls, distant and indifferent, as if it's watching her but refusing to intervene.

Yesterday still clings to her, the explosion, the shame that followed it, the way Callum had looked at her like she'd cracked something open neither of them knew how to fix. She doesn't want that here. She doesn't want him here at all.

This room is for facts.

Her mother's version of Keir has always been brutally efficient. He left. He chose music. He chose himself. There was no mystery in it, no lingering doubt. Just cause and effect, abandonment wrapped in practicality, when he chose wine, women, and music, as her mother liked to say. Not her.

But this castle refuses to be practical. To show her his reasons for never seeing her. Even if he chose wine, women, and music, that didn't mean he couldn't have come to see her.

If she is going to stay here, if she's going to endure ninety days surrounded by the echoes of a man who shaped her life by refusing to be part of it, then she needs something sturdier than memory and resentment.

She needs proof.

Paper doesn't lie.

Usually.

Keir's private office/musical storeroom smells faintly of dust and old leather, layered with something sharper underneath, ink, maybe, or the ghost of smoke long embedded in the walls. Morning light cuts through the tall windows at an angle that makes the desk gleam, not polished so much as worn smooth by use.

This room isn't staged the way the rest of the castle is. There's no attempt at grandeur, no careful curation for visitors. Old instruments lay scattered, an old desk layered with sheets of music and even some Diamond Record awards for the songs that sold over ten million sales are stacked against the wall. It's filled with mostly private junk that only a rock-n-roll star would appreciate.

It feels private.

Defensive. His own personal space.

Isla starts at the desk, methodical, as if she's cataloging evidence at a crime scene. She flips through stacks of sheet music and contracts, letters from managers and lawyers, tour schedules marked up with dates and arrows. The papers are dense with logistics and money, with signatures that mattered to everyone except her.

She resists the urge to read lyrics.

She is not here for poetry. He could pour emotion into songs by the dozen, but in the wreckage of his actual life, only Callum stands as proof he ever felt anything real.

She moves to the filing cabinets along the wall. The first drawer slides open easily, tax records, insurance documents, and correspondence with accountants. The second drawer sticks.

She yanks it harder than necessary, irritation tightening her chest.

Locked.

Of course, it is.

Her jaw tightens, but she forces herself to breathe. Anger will make her careless. Carelessness will turn this into exactly what her mother always accused her of being: emotional, impulsive, and impractical.

She kneels beside the desk and runs her fingers along the underside of the shelves. The wood is smooth where hands have brushed it again and again, worn down by habit.

Her fingers brush metal.

A key.

Her pulse jumps.

She straightens slowly, key cool and solid in her palm, and fits it into the bottom-right drawer. The lock turns with a soft, reluctant click.

Inside is order.

Not the chaotic sprawl she half expected, but careful, almost meticulous organization. Folders labeled in Keir MacLaren's handwriting. Personal correspondence set apart from business. A battered leather notebook with a strap worn soft from use, the edges darkened by years of handling.

And beneath it all—

A photograph.

Isla's breath leaves her in a rush she can't stop.

She lifts it slowly, as if the image might vanish if she moves too fast.

It's her.

Alone.

Six, maybe seven. Sitting on the steps of her mother's old house, knees pulled to her chest, hair tangled and wild, eyes bright but guarded in a way that twists something deep in Isla's chest. There's a scrape on her elbow.

She remembers that fall. She'd been chasing the neighbor's dog and tripped on the cracked concrete, furious more at herself than the pain. Her mother was angry that she'd risked an injury to her wrist.

Her mother had taken that picture.

Isla knows it instantly.

Her fingers tremble.

"Where did he get this?" she whispers.

A guitar string vibrates softly behind her.

Not loud. Not dramatic.

Just a quiet, deliberate sound that slides into the room like a breath.

Isla doesn't turn right away. She doesn't need to. The presence settles around her, solid and unmistakable.

Callum.

"You move quietly for someone carrying an instrument," she says.

"You move loudly for someone trying not to be found," he replies.

She turns.

He stands just inside the door, guitar slung over his shoulder, posture easy in a way that immediately puts her on edge. He isn't here to confront her. He isn't here to stop her.

That somehow feels worse.

"I didn't ask for help," Isla says.

"No," Callum agrees. "You didn't."

He closes the door behind him without ceremony and leans the guitar case against the wall. The movement is casual, practiced. He's done this before, in rooms like this, with people who didn't know what they were about to hear.

"Why are you here?" she asks.

He shrugs. "You weren't playing."

"That's your reason?"

"I listen when something changes."

She scoffs softly. "That sounds exhausting."

"Usually is."

She turns back to the desk, refusing to let his presence derail her focus. She's not here for him. She's not here for music.

She's here for answers.

Callum steps closer, drawn despite himself. He leans over her shoulder to see the photograph better, his arm brushing hers, his chest close enough that she can feel his warmth through her sleeve.

She hates how grounding it feels.

Hates that her body registers him before her mind can push him away. No, just no. Not with Callum, and yet the smell of him sends her pulse pounding.

"He never let anyone touch that drawer," Callum says quietly. "Ever."

Isla swallows. "That doesn't answer my question."

"No," he agrees. "But it tells you something."

She studies the photograph again. The edges are soft, worn thin from handling. This wasn't shoved into a drawer and forgotten.

"This was taken at my mother's house," Isla says. "She would never have given it to him."

Callum's jaw tightens. "Then he took it."

The word lands like a rock. When had he been at the house? Or had her mother sent it to him?

"He stole a picture of me," Isla says, disbelief sharpening her voice.

"He kept it," Callum counters.

"That's not the same thing. But as far as I knew, he never came to the house. So how did he get that photo?"

"I don't know," he says gently.

Her grip tightens around the photograph. "If he cared enough to steal and keep my picture, if he carried me with him in secret, then why didn't he come back for me?"

"I can't answer that."

"Why wasn't I enough?"

The question escapes before she can stop it.

Why keep this and still stay away?

Why look at this and never come back?

Callum doesn't answer immediately.

He's too close. She's too aware of him, the solid line of his shoulder, the faint scent of wood and strings and something uniquely him. He hasn't moved away. He hasn't reached for the photo.

He's letting her have this moment.

"I don't know," he says finally. "But I don't think indifference was the reason."

"That's not comforting."

"No," he agrees. "It's worse."

She sets the photo back in the drawer carefully, as if it might bruise if she's careless. Her hands linger there longer than necessary. Did this mean he cared and still left?

Callum straightens and steps away, giving her space. The absence of his closeness feels like a loss she resents.

He picks up the guitar.

"I'm not here to distract you," he says. "But sometimes music helps you think sideways."

She arches a brow. "That sounds like a trap."

"Probably is."

He sits on the edge of the desk, not facing her directly, and tunes the guitar with quick, efficient movements. He doesn't play one of Keir's songs. He doesn't show off.

He plays something spare.

A progression that loops and shifts, never quite resolving, leaving deliberate space between notes.

Isla listens despite herself.

"You rushed the third measure," she says automatically.

Callum glances up, surprised, and then faintly amused. "Did I?"

"Yes. You didn't let it breathe."

He slows, fingers adjusting.

The sound deepens, settles into something steadier.

"Better," she admits, then scowls at herself for saying it.

They don't talk about Keir.

They talk about restraint. About silence. About why certain notes ache while others simply exist. About how sometimes the wrong note tells the truth faster than the right one ever could.

"I hate that this works," Isla mutters.

Callum smiles faintly. "I won't tell anyone."

The moment is small. Fragile.

And dangerous.

Because for the first time since she arrived, Isla feels, just for a second, safe.

The realization takes shape inside her. When was the last time she felt truly secure?

She straightens abruptly. "This doesn't mean anything."

Callum nods easily. "Of course not."

"I'm not staying," she adds. "Not for you. Not for this."

"I know."

"You're temporary."

"So are you."

That should reassure her.

It doesn't.

Isla turns back to the desk with more force than necessary.

"This doesn't change why I'm here," she says, more to herself than to Callum. "I still need answers."

Callum doesn't argue. That, more than anything, unsettles her.

"Then keep looking," he says instead.

She opens the next drawer, the one above the photograph. Inside are folders, thicker, messier, less assembled. Receipts. Airline itineraries. Handwritten notes shoved between documents without order or apology.

"This is chaos," Isla mutters.

"He kept business clean," Callum says. "Personal things… not so much."

She flips through the papers quickly at first, scanning dates, locations. New York. London. Berlin. Paris. Always moving. Always somewhere else.

Her chest tightens.

"There are gaps," she says.

Callum leans over the desk, pointing, not touching. "Here. And here. He disappears for weeks at a time."

"Recording?"

"Sometimes."

"And the rest?"

Callum exhales slowly. "That's where the story never quite added up."

Isla stops flipping pages.

"What story?"

"The one he told everyone," Callum says. "That he was incapable of staying in one place. That he'd ruin anything he touched if he stayed too long."

Her hands still.

"That's convenient," she says bitterly. "Self-awareness as an excuse."

"That's what I used to think," Callum admits. "Now I'm not sure."

Isla looks up sharply. "What changed?"

Callum hesitates, then gestures vaguely between them. "This."

She scoffs. "You heard me play a sad song, and suddenly my father becomes complicated?"

"No," he says quietly. "You're complicated. He always was. I just never had reason to connect the two."

Isla doesn't know what to do with that. Could she be like her father in some ways?

They work in silence for a while. The kind that isn't awkward but isn't comfortable either, charged, alert. Callum reads dates aloud when something catches his attention. Isla matches them against memory, against her mother's carefully tailored timeline.

"He was in Denver when I was ten," Isla says slowly, staring at a receipt. "My mother said he was overseas that entire year."

Callum's jaw tightens. "Denver's a day's drive from where you lived then."

"A short flight," Isla adds.

They exchange a look.

Not triumph. Not vindication.

Something heavier.

She shoves the folder aside. "I don't like this."

Callum gives a humorless smile. "Neither did he, whenever facts got involved."

Isla pushes back from the desk, suddenly restless. She paces the room, arms folded tightly across her chest.

"I've spent my entire life believing one story," she says. "It's shaped everything, how I work, how I plan, how I leave before people can leave me."

Callum watches her carefully. "And now?"

"Now the story has cracks," she snaps. "And I don't know what's underneath."

He nods. "That's usually the worst part."

She stops pacing near the window, staring out at the way the trees reached for the sky. "Why are you helping me?"

Callum doesn't answer right away.

"When I was younger," he says finally, "I believed loyalty meant protecting someone's reputation at all costs."

"And now?"

"Now I think loyalty might mean telling the truth, even when it ruins the myth."

Isla turns back to him. "That could cost you the castle."

A flicker of something dark crosses his expression. "It already has."

The admission lands harder than she expects.

She moves back to the desk, slower this time, more careful. The photograph waits in the drawer like a quiet accusation. She doesn't take it out again.

Instead, she opens the leather notebook.

Keir's handwriting fills the pages, slanted, impatient, restless. Musical notations bleed into half-sentences. Ideas abandoned mid-thought.

And then—

Her name.

Isla freezes.

It isn't a dedication. It isn't poetic. Just a line in the margin:

Isla, piano here, not guitar.

Her throat closes.

Callum sees the change in her immediately. "What is it?"

She turns the notebook so he can see.

He goes still.

"He never wrote names down," Callum says quietly. "He said it made things too real."

Her fingers trace the word. "Then why write mine?"

Callum doesn't answer.

He can't.

The silence stretches, heavy and intimate. Callum steps closer without seeming to realize he's doing it, his presence warm and steady at her back. Not touching, but close enough that she feels anchored.

She hates how much she wants to lean into it.

Hates that her body reacts before her heart can harden.

"I can't do this," she says suddenly, snapping the notebook shut. "I can't rewrite my entire childhood based on scraps of paper and your memories."

Callum steps back at once. "Then don't."

She blinks. "What?"

"Don't decide anything today," he says. "Just… keep the evidence."

She studies him. "You're remarkably reasonable for someone who might lose everything."

A corner of his mouth lifts. "I've already lost worse."

She doesn't ask what.

The room settles again, quieter now, but not empty. Isla gathers the notebook and the photograph, stacking them neatly.

"I'm keeping these," she says.

Callum nods. "You should."

She hesitates, then adds, "This doesn't mean I trust you."

"I wouldn't expect you to."

"And it doesn't mean this—" she gestures vaguely between them, "—is anything."

"Of course not."

The agreement feels fragile.

Isla moves toward the door, then stops. "You know this makes things harder."

Callum meets her gaze. "The truth usually does."

She leaves the office with the weight of paper in her hands and something far heavier pressing against her ribs.

She tells herself Callum is temporary.

She tells herself the castle is just stone and history and obligation.

But as she walks away, she can still feel the warmth of him at her back, and that, more than anything Keir left behind, terrifies her.

CHAPTER 12

The phone rings while Isla is practicing scales she doesn't need.

She knows she doesn't need them. Her fingers move automatically, muscle memory honed by decades of discipline, by mornings that began before sunlight and nights that ended with her hands aching and her mind refusing to rest. Still, she plays them anyway, precise and controlled, because control is easier than thought.

The sound cuts through the music.

She ignores it once.

The second ring is sharper, more insistent, as if whoever is calling knows she's listening and refuses to be dismissed.

Isla exhales and lifts her hands from the keys. The final note hangs in the air, unfinished, before dissolving into silence.

She checks the screen.

Her mother.

Her chest tightens.

Of course, it's her mother. It's always her mother when Isla pauses long enough to be reachable. Distance has never mattered. Alisa has always known when to press.

Isla lets it ring a third time before answering.

"Hi, Mama."

"Isla." Her mother's voice is warm, controlled, perfectly pitched between concern and authority. "I was beginning to think you weren't going to answer."

"I was practicing."

A pause. Just long enough to register disapproval without voicing it.

"You've been there longer than I expected," Alisa says. "Your manager has been calling."

Isla stiffens. "I told him I was taking personal time."

"Yes," Alisa replies smoothly. "And he told me you have two performances coming up that require preparation. Commitments you don't usually neglect."

There it is. The soft blade beneath the velvet.

"I'm not neglecting anything," Isla says carefully. "I'm regrouping. And I'm preparing while I'm here."

"You don't regroup in a castle in the Highlands," her mother says lightly. "You regroup at home. With your piano. With your schedule."

With me, the unspoken words add.

Isla's fingers curl against the bench. "I'm exactly where I need to be right now."

Another pause. This one colder.

"I know this trip has been… emotional," Alisa says. "But you've stayed long enough. Ninety days is excessive for someone with your responsibilities."

Isla's spine straightens. "The will states—"

"I'm not talking about the will," her mother interrupts gently. "I'm talking about your life."

Isla closes her eyes.

This is familiar territory. Concern reframed as a command. Love wielded like leverage. Her mother has always been careful not to sound cruel. Cruelty is obvious. Control works better when it feels reasonable.

"I have rehearsals scheduled," Alisa continues. "Interviews pending. You can't disappear every time the past demands attention."

The past.

As if it's a hobby Isla indulges too often.

"I'm not disappearing," Isla says. "I'm learning."

"Learning what?" Alisa asks, and there's the faintest edge beneath the question. "He's gone, Isla. Digging through his things won't change that."

Isla's throat tightens. "You don't know that."

"I know enough," her mother says. "Enough to protect you."

Protect.

Isla remembers being ten years old, crying quietly in her bedroom while her mother told her that disappointment was a weakness she could afford exactly once. She remembers being fourteen, offered an opportunity, and warned what it would cost. She remembers being seventeen and exhausted and told that exhaustion was the price of excellence.

She remembers being told that her father had chosen music over her.

Full stop.

"I'm not a child," Isla says.

"No," Alisa agrees. "You're a woman with a career you worked very hard for. One that requires focus."

"And obedience," Isla mutters.

Her mother exhales, the sound controlled. "Isla. Don't do this."

"Do what?"

"Turn this into something it isn't."

Isla opens her eyes and stares at the piano keys, black and white and uncompromising. "What is it, then?"

"It's closure," Alisa says firmly. "And closure doesn't require excavation."

Isla's jaw tightens. "You always did prefer clean endings."

"That's because messy ones destroy people."

Isla thinks of the photograph in the drawer. The worn edges. The proof of care that had been hidden, not erased.

"Send me your flight details," Alisa says. "I'll have your assistant adjust your schedule."

"I'm not coming home yet."

Silence.

Not the polite pause of conversation. The dangerous kind.

"I beg your pardon?"

"I said I'm not coming home yet," Isla repeats, her voice steady even as her pulse races.

"Isla," her mother says, and now the warmth is gone. "This is not a negotiation."

It never has been.

"I'm staying," Isla says. "I need to finish this."

"Finish what?" Alisa demands. "He didn't come back. He's dead. End of story."

Isla's breath catches.

"Are you afraid I'll discover some hidden secret?" she asks softly.

The line goes quiet.

For one terrifying second, Isla thinks her mother has hung up.

Then Alisa speaks, and her voice is very calm.

"You're tired," she says. "You're grieving. And grief makes people reckless."

"No," Isla replies. "Loss of control does."

Another pause. This one longer.

"You're coming home," Alisa says finally. "We'll talk about this when you're thinking clearly."

"I am thinking clearly," Isla says. "For the first time in a long time."

"You're being influenced," her mother snaps. "That man—"

"Don't," Isla cuts in sharply. "Don't bring Callum into this."

"I will bring anyone into it if they are distracting you from your obligations."

There it is. The word that has governed Isla's life more than love ever has.

"I'll call you tomorrow," Alisa says, already retreating into control. "After you've calmed down."

The line goes dead.

The silence after the call is too loud.

Isla lowers the phone slowly, as if the sound might still be attached to it, as if her mother's voice might leap back out and finish the argument.

Her hand is shaking. She notices that before anything else, how her fingers tremble, how the calm she worked so hard to maintain has cracked like thin ice.

She presses the phone face down on the piano bench.

Her chest feels tight. Not panic. Not grief.

Control.

That old, familiar grip closing around her ribs.

Isla sinks down on the bench, elbows braced on her knees, staring at the floor. She breathes the way she was taught to breathe before walking onstage, slow, counted, deliberate, but it doesn't help. This isn't performance nerves. This is something older. Deeper.

She hadn't raised her voice. She hadn't cried. She hadn't agreed.

And yet she feels like she's ten years old again, standing in the doorway while her mother explains what's best for her, what's reasonable, what's necessary.

You don't need that.

You don't want that.

Trust me.

Isla presses her palm flat against her chest.

Her mother never forbade her from feeling anything outright. That would have been too obvious. Instead, she'd organized Isla's life so efficiently that feelings became inconvenient side effects, things to be managed, postponed, or quietly outgrown.

Music had been allowed because it could be shaped into discipline. Grief had been tolerated because it sharpened ambition. Anger had been redirected because it fueled excellence.

But questions?

Questions were dangerous.

Isla stands abruptly, the bench scraping softly behind her. She paces the length of the music room, bare feet whispering against stone. The castle feels different now, less like an inheritance, more like a provocation.

You've stayed long enough.

The words echo.

Her mother never said *come home because I miss you.* She said *come home because this is disruptive.*

Isla laughs softly, the sound edged and humorless.

"I won't," she says to the empty room. "Not this time."

The decision settles into her bones with surprising steadiness.

She isn't leaving. Not because of the will. Not because of Keir.

Because something here frightens her mother enough to reach across an ocean and tighten the leash.

That thought sends a sharp, electric clarity through her.

Isla grabs her sweater from the back of the chair and strides out of the room.

She doesn't hesitate. She doesn't second-guess herself.

She goes straight to Keir's office.

The office looks smaller in the late afternoon light.

Or maybe Isla is bigger now, angrier, sharper, less willing to move carefully through a space that suddenly feels complicit.

She opens the drawers she skipped earlier. Pulls folders apart with impatience. The neatness that once impressed her now irritates her. This room is not neutral. It is cultivated silence.

"This is ridiculous," she mutters, flipping through correspondence that leads nowhere.

Contracts. Royalties. Schedules.

All the proof of a life lived loudly, publicly, everywhere except where she was.

Her throat tightens.

Isla shoves one folder aside and opens another. This one thinner. Older. The paper smells faintly of dust and time. She skims quickly, irritation building.

Nothing.

Nothing.

Nothing.

The fury spikes suddenly, sharp and uncontained.

"Where are you?" she demands of the empty room.

The words come out louder than she intends.

She presses her hands flat on the desk, head bowed, breathing hard. This is exactly what her mother warned her about, this unraveling, this reckless need to *know*.

But she can't stop now.

The door creaks softly.

Callum.

Isla doesn't look up. "If you're here to tell me to slow down, don't."

"I wasn't going to," he says quietly.

She straightens despite herself. He stands just inside the doorway, watching her with an intensity that makes her chest ache in a way she doesn't want to examine.

"My mother called," Isla says. "She wants me home."

Callum's jaw tightens. "And that's why you're tearing the place apart."

"Yes." She swallows. "Because she's afraid."

Callum steps closer, drawn into the orbit of her fury. "Of what?"

"That I'll find something she couldn't control."

She gestures helplessly at the papers. "But I'm not finding it. I'm just proving what I already knew, that he chose everything else."

"That's not true," Callum says.

The certainty in his voice makes her spin toward him.

"Oh?" she snaps. "Because from where I'm standing—"

She stops.

He's close. Too close. Near enough that she can touch him, the solid steadiness of his presence in a way that makes her suddenly, painfully aware of how alone she's been.

"You don't get to tell me what's true," Isla says, her voice trembling despite her effort to control it.

"I'm not," Callum replies. "I'm saying you're looking for proof that hurts you."

She laughs sharply. "That's all there is."

"No," he says. "There's something else. You just haven't let yourself see it yet."

The room feels tight. Charged.

Isla takes a step back, bumping into the desk. Callum follows instinctively, stopping just short of touching her. His hands brace on the desk on either side of her, caging her in without trapping her.

Her breath stutters.

This is dangerous.

She should push him away. She should tell him to back off. She should remember every reason this is a bad idea, this man, this castle, this moment.

Instead, she tilts her chin up and meets his gaze.

"You don't know what I need," she says, her breath whispery soft.

Callum's voice drops. "I know what you're afraid of."

That does it.

The control snaps.

Isla surges forward and her lips land on his. They're soft, and warm, and oh God, tremors rack her body. It's been so long.

The kiss is not gentle. It's not careful. It's a collision, her mouth crashing into his, her hands fisting his shirt as if she's anchoring herself to something solid. For one heartbeat, Callum is stunned.

Then he kisses her back.

Not with restraint.

With heat.

His hands slide to her waist, firm and grounding, holding her like he understands exactly what this is, not romance, not comfort, but *release*. The kiss deepens, urgent and raw, tasting of anger and want and something dangerously close to hope.

Isla gasps against his mouth, the sound half-sob, half-laugh.

She pulls back abruptly, breathless, eyes wide.

"No," she says, shaking her head. "No, that was—"

He pulls her to him tightly, his mouth covering hers, and for a second, she relaxes against him. The feel of him hot against her has a moan escaping from her throat.

She pulls away. "We can't."

Callum stills instantly, hands dropping. "Isla—"

"That can't happen," she says, pressing her fingers to her lips as if she can erase the feeling. "I don't do this. I don't lose focus."

"You weren't losing it," Callum says softly. "You were breaking."

That terrifies her more than the kiss.

Isla turns away, heart pounding, and yanks open the next drawer.

"This means nothing," she says fiercely. "Nothing."

Callum doesn't argue, but he reaches out and rubs his hand down her back as if to reassure her.

He says quietly, "Keep looking."

She does.

And this time, this time, the evidence finally appears.

CHAPTER 13

The castle sleeps like a liar.

It looks peaceful in the early morning, mist tucked into the low places of the grounds, light softening the sharp angles of stone, the wind moving through the trees like it's only passing through. If you didn't live here, you'd think it was all old-world romance and quiet history.

Callum knows better.

History isn't quiet. It just learns to whisper.

And this morning, the whisper has a mouth and a name and the taste of citrus soap and heat, and it's the reason he's been awake since before dawn.

Isla MacLaren kissed him like she didn't care what she shattered.

Callum has replayed that mouth sucking kiss a hundred times and hated himself a hundred times for the same reason, because the moment she surged into him, his restraint broke clean in half. He didn't stop her. He didn't step back and let her recover control. He kissed her back like he'd been waiting for permission.

It wasn't romance.

It was anger. It was grief. It was a woman finally snapping under a lifetime of being managed and tugged and steered.

All of that can be true and still not change the fact that his body remembers the pressure of her mouth, the sharp hitch of her breath, the way her hands fisted in his shirt like she needed something solid to hold onto or she'd come apart completely.

He scrubs a hand over his jaw and forces himself to breathe.

It's daylight now. It's morning. He is not sixteen, not trapped in a boys' school where every choice was punishment. He is not fourteen, waiting for another adult to decide what he's allowed to want.

He is a man in a castle he has fought to keep standing.

He can make a decision.

So he does.

When he hears footsteps, fast, clipped, purposeful, he keeps his hands in his pockets. A deliberate act of self-control. A reminder that desire doesn't get to decide what happens next.

Isla enters without looking at him, a folder tucked under her arm, hair pulled back tight. She's dressed for work, clean lines, minimal fuss, a kind of composure that reads like armor. Shadows sit beneath her eyes, faint but unmistakable.

She didn't sleep either.

"Morning," Callum says.

"It is," she answers, as if the words cost her nothing.

No mention of last night. No awkwardness. No apology.

He almost prefers it to the alternative, almost.

She crosses to the long table and spreads the papers they found yesterday in Keir's office: flight searches, torn calendar pages with dates crossed out again and again, a half-completed list of requirements in Keir's handwriting that reads like a man talking himself into a life he kept postponing.

One piece of paper they found yesterday gave her hope. One simple clue that was both gratifying and infuriating. A letter from his solicitor that simply said, Alisa said now was not a good time. It appeared that Keir had tried to visit Isla, and Alisa told him not now.

"We need to organize this," Isla says. "Chronologically. Without interpretation."

Callum leans against the back of a chair. "That'll be difficult."

Her gaze flicks up, sharp. "Then don't make it harder."

He gives a shallow nod and pulls out a chair, sitting opposite her, close enough that the table feels smaller than it should.

He becomes aware of her in the way he becomes aware of a storm building, pressure, electricity, the certainty that something is going to break if the air gets heavy enough.

They start sorting.

At first, it's pure mechanics: dates, cities, torn edges fitted back together like a puzzle. Isla's hands move with precise efficiency, fingers quick and decisive. She's good at this kind of work. Not because she likes it, but because she's been trained to treat chaos as an enemy.

Callum watches her, and he hates the idea that this, sorting through the debris of Keir MacLaren's life, is something she's better at than grief.

Her phone buzzes on the table.

She ignores it.

It buzzes again.

Callum doesn't need to see the screen to know who it is.

"They're persistent," he says lightly, testing the surface.

"That's one word for it," Isla replies, not looking up.

Her phone vibrates a third time, then stops. A moment later, her email pings. Then again.

She closes her eyes for half a second, so brief, he almost misses it, then turns the screen facedown as if that can silence the world.

Callum feels something cold settle in his chest.

"You're not going to check?" he asks.

"No."

Another ping. Another.

Callum can hear the tension building under her skin. She's not calm; she's contained.

"They won't stop," he says.

Her laugh is quiet and razor-thin. "No. *They* don't."

He watches her stack the papers with more precision than necessary, like order can keep her safe.

"Who is it?" he asks anyway.

"My manager. My agent. And my mother, no doubt triangulating through both," Isla says. "They're threatening to release my performance slot. Framing it as a concern."

"Of course, they are."

"It's always a concern," she murmurs. "Concern that sounds like love until you realize it's just control wearing perfume."

The words surprise him.

He knows Isla is successful. That her life is built of airports and concert halls and applause. He's admired her discipline from a distance, the way her hands can summon something sacred from wood and ivory even before he knew she was Keir's daughter.

What he's only beginning to understand is the machinery around that success, the quiet network of people who make decisions about her life and call it support.

It looks like a cage.

They continue sorting. Callum forces his gaze to the papers, to the evidence, to anything that isn't the line of Isla's mouth. The fullness of her lips. The way she smells.

He fails when she leans forward to reach a page near his side of the table. Her arm grazes his chest as she reaches across him, and the contact, brief, accidental, hits him like a spark.

Isla stills too.

For a heartbeat, neither of them moves.

Then she withdraws her arm quickly, like she's been burned,

and resumes sorting as if she hasn't just turned the air between them into something volatile.

Callum's jaw tightens. He keeps his hands in his pockets.

Control is a choice, he reminds himself.

He makes it again.

"Here," he says, forcing his attention to the papers. "This one repeats."

He slides a page across. In the margin, in Keir's sharp handwriting, a line is repeated, small, almost hidden in the corner as if it shouldn't be read by anyone else.

If A. refuses again, wait.

Isla leans in, close enough that her shoulder nearly touches his. Callum is suddenly too aware of her heat, her scent, the way her breath shifts when she concentrates.

"A," Isla says softly. "Any idea who that is?"

Callum shakes his head. "Keir wasn't big on initials. If he used one, it was deliberate."

"So he's hiding someone."

"Or something," Callum says.

Isla sits back, lips pressed together. "'Refuses again.' That means this conversation happened before. More than once."

Callum looks at the dates and the crossed-out calendar pages. "And every time, he waited."

Isla's eyes narrow. "Why?"

Callum knows the truth. "He didn't wait unless someone forced him."

Isla's gaze snaps to his. "You sound sure."

"I am."

The silence stretches. Isla's phone pings again, and it's like the sound slices through the room and hits her in the ribs.

She flips it over, just long enough to see what's on the screen, and Callum catches a glimpse too: bold subject lines, urgent phrasing, a calendar invitation shoved into her day.

She turns it facedown again.

"Penalties," she says flatly. "If I don't confirm by the end of the week, they'll start shifting my dates. Reassigning slots."

"That's fast," Callum mutters.

"It always is," she says. "Pressure works better when it doesn't give you time to think."

Callum feels something harden inside him.

"What did your mother say?" he asks carefully.

Isla's hands pause over the papers. For the first time this morning, she looks tired rather than controlled.

"She said ninety days is excessive," Isla replies. "She said closure doesn't require excavation."

Callum's stomach tightens.

"And what did you say?"

Isla's eyes lift. "I didn't agree."

A simple sentence. A rebellion. He can hear the cost of it in the tightness of her voice.

Callum finds himself standing without realizing he's moved. The chair scrapes softly behind him.

Isla looks up, startled, and Callum realizes he's too close, on the same side of the table now, close enough that the air between them is warm.

He stops before he can reach for her.

"Is that what it's always been like?" he asks, and he hates that his voice is low, too intimate. "People deciding what you're allowed to do and calling it care?"

Isla's throat moves as she swallows. "Since I was a teenager."

The answer hits him like a fist.

Callum inhales slowly, forcing himself not to touch her. Not yet. Not unless she chooses it again.

"And you still became this," he says quietly. "You still built everything you have."

Isla's laugh is brittle and sharp. "At what cost?"

The question hangs there, raw.

Callum sees it then, clearly, without myth, without story. Isla's success isn't just talent. It's survival.

He reaches out before he can stop himself and brushes his fingers against her wrist. He feels her pulse jump under his touch.

Her eyes widen.

Callum doesn't pull away. He cups her wrist gently, thumb pressing against the inside where her skin is soft and vulnerable.

"I don't know what it cost you," he says honestly. "But it wasn't because you weren't strong enough."

Isla's breath stutters.

For a heartbeat, she leans into his hand. Just slightly. Enough that Callum's control wobbles.

The room feels smaller. Hotter. Charged.

"This is a bad idea," Isla whispers.

Callum's mouth goes dry. He doesn't deny it.

He dips his head, just slightly, close enough that his breath ghosts over her lips. Close enough that one more inch would undo both of them.

"Then tell me to stop," he murmurs.

Isla doesn't.

Her hand slides up his forearm, fingers curling into his sleeve, and Callum's heart slams hard against his ribs. For one wild second, he thinks she's going to kiss him again. Thinks he might let her. Thinks the consequences can burn later.

Then her phone buzzes.

The sound is absurdly loud in the quiet.

The spell shatters.

Isla pulls back abruptly, pressing her hand to her chest as if she's trying to reassemble the pieces of herself.

"We can't," she says, more to herself than to him. "Not now."

Callum drops his hand immediately, stepping back. The loss of contact feels like a physical blow.

"You're right," he says, forcing calm into his voice. "We focus."

Isla nods, breathing hard. "We find what he hid."

She turns back to the papers with renewed urgency, anger sharpening her movements into something fierce.

Callum follows her lead, because if he doesn't, he will reach for her again.

They search for patterns. The "A." notation appears twice more in different forms: an initial, a half-finished phrase, a line scratched out so heavily the paper thins.

"'A' must be for Alisha. That's the only person it could be."

Callum flips through Keir's battered notebook again. Music fills most of the pages, but tucked between two sections is a folded sheet of paper, yellowed and creased with age.

He unfolds it carefully.

Isla steps closer, close enough that her shoulder brushes his. She doesn't pull away this time. Neither does he.

It's a list. Short. Practical. Written in Keir's impatient hand.

Documents — north wing.

Old room. Locked.

Callum's stomach tightens.

Isla reads it, then looks at him. "There's another room."

"There used to be," Callum says. "Storage suite in the north wing. It was sealed years ago. Damp, drafty, mostly useless."

"Unless you're hiding something," Isla says.

Callum nods slowly. "Unless you're hiding something."

Isla's gaze drops to the note again, then to the "A." notation. Her mind is working fast, connecting lines.

"Keir stored legal papers elsewhere," she says, voice steady but sharp. "And he used an initial when he wrote about whoever stopped him. Mostly my mother."

Callum exhales. "Yes."

Isla's phone pings again, an email this time, the screen lighting. She doesn't look, but Callum catches the subject line: URGENT: Confirmation Needed / Contractual Obligations.

He feels something dark twist in his gut.

"They're trying to pull you back," he says.

Isla's eyes flash. "Let them try."

It's the most defiant thing she's said since she arrived.

Callum finds himself staring at her, at the fire in her expression, at the way she holds herself like she's finally choosing her own direction.

He shouldn't admire it. Admiration will turn into want too fast.

He does anyway.

"We should go," Callum says, voice rougher than he intends. "Before you change your mind."

Isla's gaze snaps to his. "I'm not going to change my mind."

Callum nods and gathers the note, tucking it carefully into the folder. When he hands it to her, his fingers brush hers. The contact is brief, but it lands like an echo.

Her breath catches.

His does too.

Neither of them speaks.

They move through the castle together, not side by side like companions, but close enough that Callum is constantly aware of her. The corridors are colder in the north wing, the stone damp with age. The air smells faintly of dust and old secrets.

Isla glances up at the high ceilings, the narrow windows, the shadows pooled in corners. "This part feels… forgotten."

"It mostly is," Callum says. "No reason to come here unless you're avoiding something."

Isla's mouth tightens. "Or looking for it."

Callum leads her down a narrower corridor, one he rarely uses, to an old tapestry that hangs heavy and faded. Behind it, half hidden, is a door.

Iron lock. Thick hinges. The kind of door that isn't meant for casual entry.

"This is it," Callum says.

Isla steps closer, studying the lock. "Keir kept this locked?"

"Always."

She turns to him. "And you never opened it."

Callum feels the question beneath her words: *Why did you respect his boundaries when he never respected mine?*

"I didn't," Callum admits. "Because it wasn't my place."

Isla's eyes search his face. "Everything in this castle is your place."

Callum swallows. "Not this."

Isla holds his gaze a moment longer, then nods once as if accepting the answer without forgiving it.

Callum pulls out the keyring Keir kept in his nightstand. He tries one key. Nothing.

Another. Still nothing.

Isla shifts impatiently, arms folded. "Of course, it wouldn't be easy."

Callum suppresses a grim smile. "Keir didn't like easy."

He pauses, then selects a thinner key, unmarked, one he almost overlooked.

It turns.

The lock gives with a soft, reluctant click.

Isla exhales like she didn't realize she'd been holding her breath.

Callum pushes the door open. It groans on old hinges, sound echoing down the corridor.

Inside, the room is dim and cold. He flicks on the light switch and it shows that dust coats everything. Shelves line the walls, stacked with boxes and trunks and old cases, the air thick with neglect. It smells of damp stone and paper left too long.

Isla steps inside slowly, reverently, as if she's entered a chapel.

"This is it," she whispers.

Callum follows, letting go of the door, which doesn't close completely.

Isla moves deeper, scanning the shelves. Her breath fogs faintly in the cold air. "He hid this well."

"He hid everything well," Callum says softly.

Isla turns, looking at him. The dim light catches in her eyes, making them look darker, more intense.

For a moment, she isn't the polished pianist or the furious heir. She's simply a daughter standing in the shadow of a father she never got to know.

Callum feels something twist in his chest.

He takes a step toward her without thinking.

Isla doesn't retreat.

They stand too close again. Close enough that Callum can feel warmth radiating off her despite the cold room. Close enough to remember her taste, the way she'd kissed him like she needed something to hold onto.

Her gaze flicks to his mouth.

Callum's throat tightens.

He should step back.

He doesn't.

The room is silent except for their breathing. For a heartbeat, Callum thinks she might kiss him again. He thinks he might let her.

Then there's a faint sound behind them.

A shift.

A soft thud.

Callum turns sharply.

The door.

It's closed, more than closed. The old latch has dropped into place completely, as if settling under its own weight. The heavy iron bolt sits flush.

Callum crosses the room and grips the handle, testing it.

It doesn't move.

He tries again, harder.

Nothing.

Isla's voice is quiet behind him. "What is it?"

Callum keeps his hand on the handle, forcing himself to stay calm. "It's stuck."

Isla steps closer. "Stuck how?"

Callum tries the lock. The key turns, but the bolt doesn't lift. Old mechanisms. Damp. Settled iron that doesn't want to move.

He swears under his breath.

Isla's breath hitches, not panic, not yet, but awareness sharpening. "We're locked in."

Callum turns to look at her. The dim light catches the line of her throat as she swallows. Her eyes are wide, but not with fear, something else.

A sudden, electric understanding.

They are alone. Trapped. In a hidden room full of Keir MacLaren's secrets.

And neither of them can pretend the tension between them doesn't exist.

Callum feels it too, the silence tightening around them, charged and dangerous.

He doesn't move closer.

He doesn't step away.

Isla doesn't either.

They stand in the cold, dusty air, staring at each other as the reality settles.

The castle has shut the door on them.

And the quiet between them is not empty.

It's loaded.

It's the kind of silence that can become a confession if either of them breathes wrong.

Callum keeps his hand on the useless door handle, jaw tight, pulse loud in his ears.

Isla's gaze drifts, just once, to his mouth, then back to his eyes.

Neither of them speaks.

Neither of them looks away.

And the click of the lock feels like the beginning of something they can no longer avoid.

"How are we going to get out?" she whispers.

The question is soft, but her voice isn't. It's low, unsteady, threaded with something that has nothing to do with fear and everything to do with the way the room has closed in on them.

"We're not," he says quietly. "Not unless we call for help."

The truth lands between them, and the worst truth follows it. He doesn't want to. Not yet. Not now.

She takes a step closer. Then another. Each one deliberate, like she's crossing a line she knows she won't uncross. The air between them tightens, charged, unforgiving.

"I feel reckless," she says, her gaze locked on his, daring him to stop her.

Callum's breath leaves him in a rough exhale. "I've been fighting that since you walked into this room."

That's all the warning she gets.

He closes the distance in a single step and kisses her, not careful, not gentle, but raw and urgent, like the truth they've both been refusing to say. His mouth crashes into hers, stealing her breath, his hands coming up as if he needs to ground himself or he'll lose control completely.

She makes a sound against his mouth, soft, broken, and grips his shirt, pulling him closer, like she's done pretending this doesn't matter.

The kiss is desperate. Unfiltered. It tastes like anger and grief and want and the terrible relief of not being alone with it anymore.

For one suspended moment, there is nothing else.

Not the lock.

Not the secrets.

Not the consequences waiting outside the door.

Only this.

Only them.

CHAPTER 14

The kiss leaves her unsteady.

Not dizzy. Not swept. Unmoored, like her spine has forgotten how to hold her upright now that her mouth has done something reckless and honest and completely unplanned.

And oh, how her body responds in ways she'd never dreamed of. Heat infuses her like a volcano spewing hot liquid fire. Her legs feel like they're made of jelly, and Callum…he's moaning, or else there is a ghost in this room with them.

Isla presses her palms to Callum's chest as she pulls back, not because she wants distance, but because if she doesn't create space, she's not sure she'll remember why she should stop at all. His heartbeat is wild beneath her hands. Too fast. Too hard.

Matching hers.

For a suspended moment, neither can talk.

The storage room is cold, stone walls sweating damp into the air, dust clinging to everything like it's been waiting, but heat coils low in her belly, sharp and unwelcome and undeniable. She tells herself it's adrenaline. The shock of being trapped. The simple physics of too much tension and too little air.

That lie lasts exactly two seconds.

She can still taste him.

She steps back first. Just one space. Enough to breathe again.

The room comes back into focus slowly.

Wooden shelves. Old trunks. Cardboard boxes stacked in uneven towers. A single bulb overhead that flickers like it's debating whether to stay alive.

"So," Isla says, folding her arms tight across her chest, "this is awkward."

Callum huffs a laugh.

The sound startles them both.

"That's one word for it," he says.

Isla's brows lift. "You're remarkably calm for someone who just trapped us in a dungeon."

"It's not a dungeon," he replies automatically. "It's a storage room."

"With one exit," Isla points out. "Which is currently refusing to acknowledge our existence."

Callum turns and grips the handle again, just to be sure. It doesn't budge.

He tries the lock. The key turns, but the bolt doesn't lift.

"Old mechanism," he mutters. "Humidity. Settling. Trapping us together."

"Of course," Isla says dryly. "Because nothing says welcome home like Victorian death traps. Did you plan this?"

Callum leans back against the door, arms folding. "Absolutely. I wanted to spend my day trapped in a storage room, with a woman who is hot one second and cold as an iceberg the next."

"There's a reason for that," she returns. "When you're pulled in all directions, you usually go a little crazy."

A chuckle escapes from him. "If it helps, this isn't how I usually host guests."

Isla snorts. The sound surprises her, laughter arriving uninvited, like a stranger who ignored the "no visitors" sign.

"I should put that in the guestbook," she says. "Five stars.

Excellent acoustics. Kidnapping potential slightly higher than expected."

His mouth twitches, and for a moment, the tension loosens, just enough for her lungs to expand fully.

The silence returns, but it's less suffocating now, more… charged.

Callum's gaze flicks to her mouth. Back to her eyes.

Isla clears her throat. "We should probably ration something."

"Ration?" Callum repeats.

She gestures vaguely. "Time. Oxygen. Sanity."

A short laugh shakes his chest. "We're not buried alive."

"Yet," Isla says. "Give the castle time."

He pushes off the door and steps farther into the room, as if movement will keep him from doing something reckless again.

"We're fine," he says. "Someone will notice eventually."

"Who?" Isla asks pointedly.

He opens his mouth, then closes it.

She lifts an eyebrow. "Exactly."

"Well," Callum says, buying time, "you could scream."

Isla considers. "I'm a professional musician. If I scream, it's usually on purpose, and people pay for tickets."

"That's… unsettlingly fair."

She gestures toward the shelves. "Besides, if I'm going to lose my mind, I'd like to do it productively."

"By digging through my mentor's secret hoard of unresolved emotional trauma?"

"Exactly."

Callum laughs again, a real laugh this time, and it fills the small space and echoes off stone. Isla freezes, staring at him.

The laugh surprises her more than the kiss did.

It's easy. Unforced. Like something he doesn't allow himself very often.

"What?" he asks, catching her look.

"Nothing," Isla says quickly. "I just… didn't expect to enjoy hearing your laughter. It's not something we've experienced in our short time together."

"Funerals have a way of stifling laughter," he admits. "Haven't had much cause lately."

Something shifts then. Not romantic. Not safe. In fact, the tension between them has shifted into a sexual energy, one she's trying to ignore.

Isla nods once, as if accepting that they're both more frayed than they want to admit.

She moves toward the shelves. "Help me."

They kneel, side by side, and Isla becomes painfully aware of how close they are again, his knee almost touching hers, his shoulder brushing hers when he reaches for a box.

She opens the first one and finds a tangle of cables.

She holds up the mess like it might bite her. "What is this?"

Callum squints. "I think that was an attempt at organized chaos."

Isla drops it back into the box. "Ah. A family tradition. Put it in a box if you don't know what to do with it."

"That was Keir. The original hoarder."

Callum laughs, really laughs, hand braced on his knee. Isla laughs too, surprised and helpless, the sound bubbling up before she can stop it.

When the laughter fades, they're both still smiling.

Still kneeling too close.

Callum wipes his eyes. "I forgot he was ridiculous sometimes."

Isla sobers slightly. "I never knew."

The weight creeps back in, softer now, but it doesn't crush. Not when laughter has cracked the seal.

They move to another box. Isla lifts the lid and recoils.

"Oh no."

"What?" Callum asks.

She pulls out a jacket that should never have existed: sequined, shredded, aggressively eighties.

"Please tell me this is not real."

Callum groans. "Oh God. He wore that onstage once. I remember my father giving him shit about dressing like he was Elvis."

"Once?" Isla demands. "This thing should come with a warning label."

"He said it 'captured the era.'"

"It captured a crime," Isla says. "Enough sequins to explain several questionable career choices."

Callum bursts out laughing again, loud enough that it echoes around them. Isla laughs too, covering her mouth with her hand, shocked at herself.

For a moment, she forgets she's locked in a room. Forgets the castle. Forgets the will. It's just her and Callum locked together, having fun.

Then her laughter dies, and the truth slams back in.

Keir is dead.

And all she has are boxes.

Isla drops the jacket back into its box and presses her hands against her thighs to steady herself.

"Okay," she says, voice tighter now. "What else did you hide, Keir MacLaren?"

Callum shifts beside her. "If he's half as dramatic as he liked to think he was, this won't be subtle."

"Good," Isla mutters. "I'm not in the mood for subtle."

They open the next box together.

At first, it's harmless: old programs, laminated backstage passes, crumpled set lists. Isla flips through them, recognizing venues, dates, the shape of a life lived in motion.

Then her fingers catch on something thicker.

A bundle wrapped in tissue paper.

Her stomach tightens, instinct warning her before her brain catches up.

She unwraps it carefully.

Photographs.

Not glossy publicity shots. Not images meant for fans or magazines.

Candid.

Private.

Her breath catches as she lifts the stack, fingertips brushing curled edges and brittle corners. The paper is thicker than modern prints, the colors slightly faded.

A life preserved.

She sinks to the floor without realizing she's done it, legs folding beneath her. Callum shifts, crouching beside her, close enough that his warmth touches her in the cold air, but he doesn't reach for her.

Doesn't rescue.

He just stays.

Isla flips the first photo.

Keir, younger than she has ever seen him. His hair darker, his face less carved by exhaustion, his smile, God, his smile is easy. Real.

His arm is slung around a woman with dark hair and sharp eyes.

Alisa.

Isla's chest tightens. She hates how her first instinct is to search her mother's face for power even in a photograph. Alisa is smiling. Radiant. Triumphant.

Keir is looking at her like she's the center of the room.

Isla flips to the next.

A wedding photo.

Formal. Bright. Her mother in a gown that glows against the darker background. Keir in a suit that looks like it cost more than Isla's first apartment.

Alisa's smile is wide, shining, almost victorious.

Keir looks… different.

Not distant. Not lost. His gaze is fixed on Alisa with something like awe, as if he can't quite believe she's real.

Isla stares at it longer than she means to.

"He looks happy," she says, the words slipping out before she can stop them.

Callum studies the photo. "He was," he says quietly. "For a while. My father said they were in love, until Keir's demons got in the way and Alisa had enough."

The quiet agreement in his voice is oddly destabilizing. Not defense. Not blame. Just fact.

Isla nods, throat tight, and turns the photo over. Another slides free beneath it.

Alisa again, standing alone in a garden, one hand resting protectively over a barely rounded stomach.

Pregnant.

Isla's breath shudders. She studies her mother's face, the way she stands, as if she already knows she's holding something the world will have to orbit.

And suddenly, Isla sees herself not as an abstract child, not as a future, but as a possession.

A gift.

A weapon.

Her fingers tighten around the photograph.

She forces herself to keep going.

The next picture steals the air from her lungs.

Hospital room. Harsh lighting. A narrow bed.

Keir sits on the edge of it, shoulders hunched, cradling something small and wrapped in white. His face is turned downward, reverent, stunned.

In his arms—

Isla.

Her vision blurs so quickly, it shocks her. Tears spill before she can stop them, hot against her cheeks, humiliating in their honesty.

She presses a hand to her mouth, as if she can hold the sound inside.

Keir's expression in the photograph is nothing like the man she's imagined her entire life. There's no distance. No avoidance.

His face is soft with wonder, eyes dark and intent as he studies the tiny bundle in his arms like she's the most fragile, miraculous thing he's ever seen.

Like he can't look away.

Callum inhales sharply beside her.

"That," he says slowly, voice rough, "is not the look of a man who never wanted to see his daughter again."

Isla's throat tightens painfully.

She can't speak. She can barely breathe.

All the stories she's carried, careful explanations, tidy conclusions, the narrative her mother fed her so she could swallow the past without choking, fracture under the weight of this single image.

He held me.

He looked at me like I mattered.

Isla swipes at her cheeks angrily, furious with herself for crying, furious that she can feel the grief of a moment she never remembered.

"It doesn't make sense," she whispers. "None of it does."

Callum shifts closer. Not touching. Just close enough that his presence steadies the air.

"No," he agrees softly. "It doesn't."

Isla clutches the photograph to her chest, pressing its corners against her sternum like it can anchor her. Like proof can replace memory.

The castle presses around them, stone and silence and secrets, too solid, too old, too full of things that were never spoken.

And the kiss still hums in her blood.

That's what terrifies her most.

Because she is not only unraveling in front of Callum, she is *aware* of him in a way she has never allowed herself to be aware of any man. She notices the way he watches her. The way his breathing changes when she cries. The way he looks at the photograph like he wants to destroy whoever made that moment end.

Isla squeezes her eyes shut.

This is not safe.

Nothing here is safe.

Not the past.

Not the truth.

Not Callum.

She draws a shaky breath and forces her voice steady. "If he felt that… then why—"

Callum's answer is quiet but firm. "Something happened. Something stole him away from your mother. Maybe it's time she answered some questions."

Isla opens her eyes and looks at him, the tears drying on her cheeks, anger building beneath the grief.

"My mother told me the story was finished," she says. "End of story. He didn't come back."

Callum's gaze hardens. "And yet…"

She holds up the photograph again, shaking slightly. "And yet."

The room feels smaller. The locked door at their backs feels heavier. The shelves feel like they're leaning in, waiting.

Isla stares at the photograph of Keir holding her. Staring down at her like she was something sacred.

Then she looks at Callum. His eyes are on her with an intensity that makes her breath catch again.

The past is between them.

The castle is between them.

And still—her body remembers his mouth.

"Fine," she says, voice hoarse. "Then we keep looking."

Callum nods.

They return to the boxes with renewed purpose, the laughter gone but something else in its place now, something sharper. Determination.

Isla opens another box and finds more photographs, more fragments of a life she was never allowed to witness. Keir laughing with his bandmates. Keir in a studio, headphones around his neck. Keir leaning over a mixing board, face focused, eyes alive.

Alive.

The word slices through her.

Then she finds something folded beneath the photos: a thin envelope, unsealed, with Keir's handwriting on the front.

Not her name.

Not Alisa's.

Just a single letter.

A.

Isla's pulse stutters.

Callum's gaze snaps to it. "That's…"

"I know," Isla whispers.

She turns it over with trembling fingers.

It isn't open.

It isn't read.

It's just there, like a final breadcrumb, like a dare.

Isla looks up at Callum. "Again, we have the letter A."

Callum's expression is grim. "Someone who mattered enough to stop him. Honestly, I think it's your mother."

Isla's stomach twists. Alisa.

She grips the envelope until the paper bends slightly. "We're not leaving this room until we know what this is."

Callum's voice is low. "Then we better figure out how to get out first."

Isla glances toward the door again. The lock sits there, silent, indifferent.

The castle isn't giving them an easy escape.

Of course, it isn't.

Isla draws in a slow breath and steadies herself. "Call for help," she says. "But not my mother. Not my manager. Not anyone connected to… them."

Callum nods once, as if he understands exactly what she means.

He reaches for the door again, testing the handle, then the lock, jaw clenched.

Isla watches him, the way his shoulders tense, the way his hands flex with frustration.

And without warning, she laughs softly.

Callum turns. "What?"

She holds up the sequined jacket again, waving it like a flag. "If we die in here, I want it known that your father once wore this voluntarily."

Callum's lips twitch. "Keir wasn't my father."

Isla lifts an eyebrow. "Apparently, he had questionable taste."

Callum snorts, laughter breaking through his grimness for one breath. "God help us, you're right."

Isla's smile fades as quickly as it arrives.

She looks down at the photograph in her hand, at Keir's face as he stares down at newborn Isla like the world has shifted.

Then she looks at Callum.

The warmth from the kiss is still there, hovering under her skin like a bruise.

"You said that isn't the look of a man who never wanted to see his daughter again," she says quietly.

Callum meets her gaze, steady and certain. "It's not."

Isla's voice trembles. "Then someone stole that from me."

Callum's jaw tightens. "Yes."

The room falls silent again.

Not empty silence.

Loaded.

The kind that shifts the air, changes the shape of everything.

Isla presses the photograph to her chest once more and closes her eyes.

She isn't leaving the castle.

Not now.

Not until she knows exactly who decided her father's love was not enough.

And why.

CHAPTER 15

The storage room grows quieter the longer they stay in it.

Not empty, never empty, but hushed in the way old places get when they're listening. The walls hold sound differently here, swallowing words instead of echoing them back, as if the castle itself is deciding which truths are worth repeating.

Callum shifts his weight, careful not to brush against Isla. The proximity is dangerous. Not because of the kiss, though that still burns in his mind, but because of everything that followed it. The quiet. The way neither of them pretended it hadn't mattered.

That kiss, he felt certain, had scorched his clothing, and he just couldn't see it yet.

Callum has lived most of his adult life managing distance. Knowing how close to stand. When to pull back. When to stay silent rather than risk the wrong thing slipping out.

This room makes that discipline harder.

Isla kneels at one of the lower shelves, methodical again, her spine straight, shoulders squared. She's rebuilt herself since the kiss. He recognizes the change now, the way she locks emotion behind precision. Control as armor. Ignoring him and focusing on the mission at hand.

He doesn't interrupt.

She opens another box and sighs. "This is absurd."

Callum crouches nearby, resting his forearms on his knees. "What is?"

"Receipts. Storage invoices. Repairs from twenty years ago." She flips through the papers, irritation sharp in every movement. "Why bring this up here? Why hide it?"

"Keir didn't hide things because they were valuable," Callum says. "He hid them because they were a part of him."

She shoots him a look. "That's not comforting."

"It's not meant to be."

She snorts softly, then reaches deeper into the box. Her fingers still.

Callum feels the shift instantly. Her breath catches, not sharply, but like something inside her has gone rigid.

"What?" he asks.

She doesn't answer at first. Slowly, she pulls out a folded sheet of paper. Thicker than the rest. Official.

She opens it.

Callum leans in, scanning automatically. Header. Date. Clinic name.

Then the word.

VASECTOMY

His stomach drops. A week after her birth.

Isla stares at the paper like it's written in another language. "That's not possible."

Callum swallows. "It is."

Her head snaps up. "Why would he do that?"

The question slices through the room, sharp and demanding. Not grief yet. Anger. The kind that wants a reason, it can tear apart.

Callum can't answer. Because everything he knows about Keir suddenly feels… insufficient.

She presses the paper toward him. "Why?"

"I don't think it was about not wanting a child," he says slowly.

Her laugh is harsh. "That's exactly what it looks like."

"It looks like a man closing a door," Callum says. "But not necessarily because he didn't want what was on the other side."

"That's generous," Isla snaps.

"I'm not trying to be generous."

"Then be honest." Her voice tightens. "Why would he take a permanent step like this?"

Callum exhales, long and controlled. "Because Keir often said he believed he ruined people."

Isla's anger stutters, but only for a moment. "That's not an answer."

"It's the only one I have," he says. "He talked about failure like it was inevitable. Like once you crossed a certain line, all you could do was make things worse."

She stands abruptly. "So his solution was to get a vasectomy. And then to disappear?"

"Yes."

"That's not protection," she snaps. "That's abandonment. Just like my mother said."

Callum doesn't argue. The word fits too cleanly.

"He doesn't get to decide that for everyone else," Isla continues, pacing now, the invoice shaking in her hand. "He doesn't get to decide what kind of pain is acceptable."

Callum's chest tightens. She isn't wrong, and knowing that feels like betrayal anyway.

"I'm not defending it," he says quietly.

She stops pacing and turns to him. "Then why are you still trying to make it make sense?"

The answer costs him more than he expects. "Because if it doesn't… then everything I thought I knew about him collapses."

Silence stretches.

Isla's expression softens just slightly. "Welcome to the club. So far, none of this makes sense."

"No," he agrees, wondering how it felt to be the child of a very talented musician with lots of money, but no love from her father.

She sinks onto one of the old trunks, shoulders slumping. "This doesn't feel impulsive," she says. "It feels calculated."

"Yes," Callum agrees. "Keir didn't do anything impulsive with his body. Or his consequences."

"So something pushed him here."

Callum hesitates. "Or someone."

Her jaw tightens. "My mother always said he didn't want a family."

"That's not the same as not wanting people," Callum replies.

She looks at him sharply. "What's the difference?"

"The difference," he says carefully, "is believing you are the problem."

Her voice trembles. "That still doesn't make it right."

"No," he agrees. "It doesn't."

They sit with that. With the weight of it. With the knowledge that the truth is not going to be kind to either of them.

Finally, Isla folds the invoice carefully, as if it might shatter if she isn't gentle. "One day," she says, "I'm going to know exactly why he made this choice."

Callum nods. "And when you do, it won't erase what it cost you."

She meets his gaze. "No. But I'm going to talk to my mother and ask her if she knew about the vasectomy."

"Good idea," he says, doubting that her mother will ever tell her the truth.

The lock rattles faintly as the building settles.

"It's getting late. We need to find a way out," Isla says.

"I know."

"There's one more option," he says. "Mrs. Calder."

"The housekeeper?"

"She's been here longer than anyone. If anyone knows how to free an old lock, it's her."

Isla nods. "Call her."

Picking up his cell phone, he dials the housekeeper's line. It rings twice.

"Calder residence."

"Mrs. Calder, it's Callum. We're… indisposed."

A pause. "Indisposed how?"

"We're locked in the north wing storage room."

Another pause. Longer.

"Well," she says dryly, "that's unfortunate."

"Could you bring the master key?"

"I'll bring the hammer," she replies. "Be there shortly."

The line goes dead.

Isla exhales. "I like her."

"She terrifies me," Callum admits.

They wait in silence.

Callum watches Isla, how she steadies herself, how she refuses to let grief take over. He realizes something then that unsettles him more than the invoice ever could.

He still loves Keir.

But he no longer trusts him.

The sound of footsteps approaches. Metal scrapes. A sharp crack.

The door swings open, light spilling in.

Mrs. Calder stands there, unimpressed. "Next time," she says briskly, "leave the archaeology to professionals."

Callum steps aside to let Isla pass, watching her carefully.

As they leave the room behind, he knows with certainty that nothing they uncovered today will let either of them walk forward unchanged.

And that whatever comes next will ask them to choose between loyalty and truth.

CHAPTER 16

The call comes at the exact moment Isla can no longer pretend she won't make it.

Late afternoon in Scotland. The sky has that pale, indecisive light that never quite commits to evening this far north. Dinner hour approaching. The hour when people settle into routines and expect answers.

Five hours earlier in Long Island, New York. Isla had loved growing up in Colorado, but when her career took off, her mother moved to Long Island to be closer to her.

Early evening. Prime time for control.

Isla stares at her phone for a long moment before picking it up, already knowing what voice will greet her on the other end. Her mother has impeccable timing. Always has. She waits until resistance weakens, until exhaustion dulls the sharpest edges.

She answers on the fourth ring.

"What time does your flight land, and I'll order you a car," her mother says immediately, brisk and efficient, as if the decision has already been made.

No greeting. No inquiry about how Isla is doing. No acknowledgment that she might not comply.

Assumption, spoken aloud.

Isla closes her eyes and exhales slowly. "I'm not coming home yet."

There's a pause, fractional, controlled, but Isla hears it. The smallest hitch, like a chess player realizing the board has shifted.

"Isla," her mother says, tone smoothing instantly, "you have obligations. You need to come home."

Irritation floods Isla, hot and fast.

"Yes," she says coolly. "I've heard from my manager. He's threatening to pull contracts."

Her mother exhales sharply. "Then you understand the seriousness of the situation."

"You got to him, didn't you?" Isla presses. "Get her home right now. I'm beginning to think you're afraid of what I'll find here, and that's why you're insisting I come home."

The silence on the other end is no longer controlled.

Her mother gasps. "That is a ridiculous accusation."

"Is it?" Isla asks quietly. "Because it's starting to feel like every time I dig up something inconvenient, you tighten the leash."

"You paid your respects to your father," Alisa snaps. "But now it's time to get back to your life. Your career."

There it is.

Not *family*.

Not *grief*.

Career.

Isla straightens, pacing the length of the suite. The room is vast, with stone walls, heavy curtains, and furniture chosen by someone who understood permanence. She has slept here for two weeks and still hasn't touched half of it.

Maybe that says everything.

"Maybe it's time to stop dancing around it," Isla says.

There's a warning in her tone, and for the first time, her mother hears it.

"Mother," Isla continues evenly, "did you know that Keir got a vasectomy a week after I was born?"

The gasp on the other end is loud enough that Isla pulls the phone slightly away from her ear.

"How did you learn about that?" her mother demands.

No denial.

Just panic.

"I found the receipt in his papers," Isla says. "Why, Mother? Why would he get a vasectomy?"

She waits.

The silence stretches long enough that Isla can picture her mother, standing in some elegant kitchen, phone pressed to her ear, mind racing through versions of the truth to decide which one might still work.

Finally—

"I had a very hard labor and delivery," her mother says tightly. "Keir was with me the entire time, but watching me suffer... it got to him. I was in labor for nearly twenty-four hours. They should have given me a C-section, but the doctor just *knew* you were about to deliver."

Isla closes her eyes.

She's heard parts of this story before. The long labor. The incompetent doctor. The suffering. That much has always been true.

"Don't ever use a country doctor who should have retired years ago," her mother adds bitterly.

It fits. Too well to dismiss.

"In true Keir fashion," Alisa continues, "he reacted emotionally, without coming to talk to me. He did it without telling me. When he came home in pain, that was the first time I knew what he'd done."

Isla swallows.

"I wanted more children," her mother says, voice tight with old rage. "I wanted us to have a family. And yet he ended that possibility without discussing it with me."

Isla can understand that anger. A decision like that should never be unilateral.

"That was probably the beginning of the end," Alisa continues. "Then, when he went on tour the next time, he didn't have to worry about getting anyone pregnant. And when I surprised him, when I brought you to visit him, I found him drunk, in bed with two of his groupies. That was the final straw."

That part Isla has heard before.

It lands differently now, weighted by everything else.

"So," her mother says crisply, "now that you know the truth, it's time for you to come home."

Isla stops pacing.

"No," she says simply. "Not yet. The ninety days are not up. I'll be home when I'm finished and feel satisfied I've learned the truth about my father."

"Isla, your next concert is in sixty days."

"I'm preparing," Isla replies. "Every day I practice on his Steinway. It's a very nice piano."

The silence that follows is dense. Dangerous.

She can hear the anger seething through the phone lines.

"Is there anything else you want to tell me?" Isla asks calmly. "Before I discover it in his personal papers?"

She gives her mother an opening.

A chance.

"You know everything," Alisa says sharply. "Your father was a cheater who I kicked out of our home. His music was more important than you or I ever were."

Why does it feel like she's holding something back?

Is it the anger? The urgency? Or the way she hasn't once asked Isla how she's doing, only when she's leaving?

"Well," Isla says, voice steady, "I'm going to continue digging in my spare time, trying to learn who my sperm donor actually was. When the ninety days are up, I'll put the castle on the market and return home. In the meantime," she adds, "I'll be practicing for the concert."

There's a long silence.

"You need to call your manager," her mother finally says. "He's not happy with you."

"He's my employee," Isla replies coolly. "Not the other way around. But then again, I've always thought *you* were my manager, and Henry was just your workhorse."

The sharp intake of breath tells Isla she's hit something vital.

"And Isla," her mother adds suddenly, voice shifting, "I don't like that man."

Isla stills.

"What man?" she asks.

"You know exactly who I mean. Callum Fraser."

There it is.

Fear.

Not concern. Not dislike.

Fear.

"Why?" Isla asks softly.

"He's dangerous," her mother says. "He's filling your head with nonsense."

"He hasn't said anything about you," Isla replies.

"That's worse," Alisa snaps. "Men like him don't need to."

Isla's fingers tighten around the phone.

"Good night, Mother," she says evenly.

"I don't like what Scotland is doing to you."

"What is that supposed to mean?"

"It's changing you," her mother says.

"It's called independence," Isla replies. "I'm finally learning to live my life on my own. And I am beginning to really like Callum. He kisses like the devil."

A gasp on the other end of the line has her smiling.

She ends the call before her mother can respond.

The silence after the call feels different from before.

Not empty.

Alert.

Isla lowers the phone slowly, her fingers still curved around it like she expects it to ring again. Her mother has always had a way of reclaiming space even after conversations ended, lingering in Isla's head, rewriting what was said, reminding her who held the power.

Not this time.

This time, something has shifted.

Callum.

The realization lands fully formed, so sharp, it almost makes her laugh.

Her mother isn't afraid of the castle. Or Scotland. Or even the truth, not really.

She's afraid of Callum.

Isla sinks down onto the edge of the bed, pressing her palms to her knees as she lets that idea unfold. It explains too much. The urgency. The pressure. The way her mother's tone had changed the instant Callum's name entered the conversation.

Men like him don't need to say anything.

What did that mean?

Callum hasn't filled Isla's head with anything. If anything, he's done the opposite, held back, stepped aside, refused to lead her anywhere she didn't already intend to go. He hasn't defended Keir blindly, but he hasn't attacked him either. He's let the evidence speak, even when it cost him.

That's what makes him dangerous.

He doesn't control the narrative.

He lets it unravel.

Isla leans back against the cushions and closes her eyes, uninvited memories surfacing, the feel of Callum's mouth against hers in the storage room, the way his hands had come up like instinct rather than intent, the split second where she'd felt completely unguarded.

Not because he took anything.

Because he waited.

Her mother would hate that.

Alisa has always understood power as something you apply, not something you allow. She directs, schedules, manages, and anticipates. Isla has lived her entire life inside that current, moving forward because the water carried her there.

Callum is still water.

Unmovable.

Observant.

And Isla realizes something else, something colder.

Callum knows things her mother assumed died with Keir.

Not specifics. Not yet. But truths of character. Of pattern. Of fear.

If her mother believed Keir didn't want a family, Callum's very existence contradicts that. He is living proof that Keir showed up for his best friend's son. That he stayed. That he committed.

Isla opens her eyes slowly.

That is why her mother wants her home.

Not because Isla is in danger.

Because Alisa is…

A knock sounds softly at her bedroom door.

Isla's heart jumps before she can stop it.

She stands, smoothing her hands down the front of her sweater, irritated with herself for the reflex. She crosses the room and opens the door.

Callum stands on the threshold, his expression cautious, unreadable.

"Mrs. Calder said you were in here," he says. "I wanted to check on you."

Of course, he did.

"Did she?" Isla replies lightly, stepping back to let him in.

Callum enters, closing the door behind him with deliberate

care. He doesn't invade the space. He doesn't hover. He stands near the window, hands loose at his sides, like he's braced for whatever version of Isla he's about to encounter.

She studies him in the fading light, the lines of his face softened by dusk. He looks tired. Not just physically, emotionally, like someone who has spent the day absorbing truths he didn't ask for.

"My mother called," Isla says.

His jaw tightens. "I assumed."

"She wants me home," Isla continues. "Immediately."

"I also assumed that."

She crosses her arms. "She asked about you."

That gets his attention.

"What did she say?" Callum asks carefully.

Isla watches his face as she answers. "That she doesn't like you."

A corner of his mouth lifts, humorless. "I'm devastated."

"She said you're dangerous."

The humor vanishes.

Callum's gaze sharpens, something alert flickering behind his eyes. "Did she say why?"

"No," Isla admits. "But she didn't need to."

Callum exhales slowly. "People who rely on control don't like variables."

"And you're a variable," Isla says.

"I'm inconvenient," he corrects. "There's a difference."

She studies him for a long moment. "You knew she would react like this."

"Yes."

"And you didn't warn me."

"No."

"Why?"

Callum hesitates, then meets her gaze fully. "Because you didn't need more voices in your head."

The answer hits harder than she expects.

Isla looks away first.

"My mother thinks you're filling my head with nonsense," she says quietly.

"Am I?" Callum asks.

"No," Isla says immediately. "You're doing the opposite. You're letting me think."

Callum nods once. "That's usually enough."

She turns back to him, frustration simmering. "Why didn't he tell you about me?"

The question is raw, unfiltered.

Callum doesn't flinch. "I don't know."

"But he trusted you," Isla presses. "He raised you."

"Yes."

"So why not me?" Her voice cracks despite her control. "Why was I the thing he kept hidden?"

Callum swallows. "Because you weren't a secret," he says quietly. "You were a wound."

The words settle heavily between them.

Callum continues, slower now. "Keir hid the things he couldn't fix. Not because they didn't matter, but because they mattered too much."

Isla presses her lips together, absorbing that. "That doesn't make it better."

"No," Callum agrees. "It makes it tragic."

Silence stretches.

Outside, the sky deepens toward evening. Somewhere below, the castle settles with a soft groan, like an old animal shifting in its sleep.

"My mother thinks Scotland is changing me," Isla says eventually.

Callum watches her closely. "Is it?"

"Yes," Isla admits. "But not the way she thinks."

He waits.

"It's making me see how small my world has been," Isla says. "How carefully managed. How little of it was actually mine."

Callum's voice is low when he answers. "That tends to happen when you stop running."

She meets his gaze, something unspoken tightening between them again.

"Don't do that," Isla says softly.

"Do what?"

"Look at me like that."

Callum exhales, turning slightly toward the window. "Then don't say things that make it hard not to."

Her pulse jumps.

They stand there, the space between them charged but restrained, like the storage room all over again, only this time, the door is open, and neither of them is leaving.

Finally, Isla breaks the tension. "I realized something after the call."

"What?"

"I've never been inside Keir's bedroom."

Callum turns back to her, surprise flickering across his face. "Never?"

"Not once," Isla says. "And if this castle is a map of his secrets… then I've been avoiding the most obvious place."

Callum considers that. "Are you ready for that?"

"No," Isla says honestly. "But I wasn't ready for any of this."

She moves toward the door, resolve hardening with every step.

"Will you come with me?" she asks.

Callum doesn't answer immediately. Then: "Yes."

No conditions. No control.

Just presence.

And Isla realizes, with startling clarity, that whatever she finds next will not just change how she sees her father. It could also change how she sees her mother.

CHAPTER 17

Keir's bedroom is nothing like Isla expects.

There is no chaos here. The space feels controlled, refined, even. The bed is neatly made, the coverlet smoothed flat. The dresser top is bare except for a single lamp and a watch placed with care. Heavy curtains frame the tall windows, drawn back just enough to let in the pale Scottish light.

The room feels… held together.

Isla stands just inside the doorway, fingers curling slowly at her sides.

"This doesn't look like someone who lived recklessly and didn't care," she says quietly.

Callum steps in behind her. He doesn't say anything at first. His gaze moves slowly over the room, as if he's taking inventory of something familiar and unsettling at the same time.

"No," he says finally, "it doesn't."

They stand there together, letting the silence settle. Isla hadn't realized how much she expected anger to live here, some echo of chaos, some proof that her mother's version of Keir had been right all along.

Instead, this room contradicts everything.

She crosses to the dresser and opens the top drawer. Shirts folded with precision. Not fashionable. Practical. Neutral colors. Things meant to last.

"He was orderly," Isla murmurs.

Callum nods. "He needed things to make sense. If the outside world didn't… this did."

Isla looks up at him. "You should have been his child."

"We lived together for a long time." Callum's mouth curves faintly. "He talked. More than people think."

She opens the next drawer, socks, belts, a watch nestled in its box.

"Did he ever mention a wife in Colorado?" she asks before she can stop herself.

Callum stills.

He doesn't look away. That alone feels like kindness.

"No, he didn't speak of your mom around me. He talked about regret," he says carefully. "About mistakes that couldn't be fixed with money or apology, but he never mentioned Alisa by name."

Not an answer. But not avoidance either.

Isla nods once. "That sounds like him."

They move around the room, falling into an unspoken rhythm. She checks the nightstand. Callum scans the bookshelf along the far wall. It's filled with music, scores, theory books, and thick notebooks filled with handwritten notes.

Callum pulls one down and flips it open. His fingers linger on the pages.

"He annotated everything," he says. "Couldn't leave a thought unfinished."

Isla watches him, struck by how different he seems here. Less guarded. More… present. As if this room strips something away from him too.

"What did he teach you?" she asks.

Callum hesitates. Then, quietly, "How to survive."

That makes her look up.

"That's not music," she says.

"It was," he replies. "Just not the kind people clap for."

She waits.

Callum exhales and sets the book down. "After my father died in a small plane crash, my mother remarried. Quickly."

Isla sits on the edge of the bed, instinctively still.

"I didn't fit into the new picture," Callum continues.

Her chest tightens. "What did she do?"

"She sent me to a boys' school," he says flatly.

Something in his tone makes her heart drop.

"Boarding school?" she asks.

He shakes his head. "Correctional. Supposed to straighten me out. Discipline. Structure."

"How old were you?"

"Fourteen."

Isla's breath catches. "That's… young."

"Yes."

"Was it bad?" she asks, already knowing the answer.

Callum lets out a slow breath. "It was hell."

The word hangs between them.

"They called it character building," he continues. "But it was mostly about breaking you down until you stopped being inconvenient."

Isla's fingers curl into the bedspread. "Your mother knew?"

"She told herself it was for my own good," he says. "That I'd thank her one day."

Her voice is tight. "Did you?"

"No."

He looks at her now, fully. "Keir found out."

"How?"

"I wrote him a letter," Callum says. "Didn't even know if he'd get it. Just needed someone to know I was there."

Isla swallows hard.

"He showed up," Callum says. "Unannounced. Walked into the headmaster's office like he owned the place."

A flicker of something, pride, disbelief, moves across his face.

"He didn't argue. He didn't negotiate. He told them I was leaving. That I was his responsibility now."

Isla's eyes sting. "Just like that?"

"Just like that."

"And your mother?"

"She was furious," Callum said with a smile. "Said Keir was interfering. That I needed discipline."

"What did Keir say?"

Callum's mouth tightens. "He said discipline without compassion was cruelty."

Isla closes her eyes.

"He took me home," Callum continues. "Taught me music. Gave me work. Made me feel… salvageable. Told me my father would be proud of me. That meant a lot to me."

A silence falls, heavy and reverent.

"He stayed for you," Isla says softly.

"Yes."

The words change something between them.

Isla stands abruptly, needing motion, and crosses to the small desk near the window. She opens drawers one by one, paper, envelopes, things kept because they mattered.

"I'm happy for you" she says quietly.

The remark is clearly sarcastic.

"Yes," Callum agrees.

She turns back to him, startled. "You don't defend him."

"I don't need to," he says. "Understanding isn't absolution. We don't know why Keir didn't come to see you. If he rescued me, why wouldn't he see his own daughter?"

Isla stands at the desk, fingers still curled around the drawer edge, while Callum remains near the bookcase, his posture tight as if he's braced for the room to fight back. The story he just told sits between them, heavier than any object in Keir's bedroom.

"Have you ever told anyone how Keir saved you?" Isla says quietly.

Callum's gaze flicks to hers. "There wasn't much point."

"That's not true." Isla's voice firms.

He gives a short, humorless laugh. "I'm not sure why I told you. Maybe because I wanted you to know me and why I feel so protective of Keir."

Isla steps away from the desk, moving toward the shelves where the notebooks sit. She picks up one of Keir's annotated scores and flips through it, pretending her hands are steady.

"Maybe because you're tired of carrying it alone," she says.

Callum's jaw tightens, but he doesn't deny it.

They drift back into the search, but it feels different now, less like an invasion and more like a joint excavation. Isla checks the nightstand again, more carefully this time, lifting the lamp and running her fingers along the underside.

Callum watches her, then mirrors the motion on the other side of the room, sliding a hand along the back panel of the bookcase.

"You're thorough," he murmurs.

"I'm stubborn," Isla corrects.

"That too."

She glances at him. "Keir taught you to be observant."

"He taught me to assume people hide what matters," Callum says.

That lands like a key turning in a lock. What had he hidden?

Isla moves to the wardrobe and opens it again, not looking at the clothes this time but at the structure, hinges, seams, edges. She presses against the back panel.

It doesn't move.

Callum crosses the room and stops beside her, close enough that she feels his heat. Not touching. Just there.

"Try the bottom," he says.

"Why?"

"Because Keir always hid things where people didn't want to kneel," Callum replies.

Isla snorts, then crouches, fingertips brushing the baseboard. She finds a narrow seam she missed before. A slight gap.

Her pulse jumps.

"There," she whispers.

Callum drops to a crouch beside her. "Good eye."

Together they press along the seam. The panel shifts, barely, but enough to reveal a shallow compartment. Isla sucks in a breath.

"Of course," she mutters. "A hidden compartment. Because why be normal when you can be Keir MacLaren?"

Callum's mouth twitches. "He'd consider normal an insult."

Isla reaches inside. Her fingers brush paper. A small bundle of folded documents. She pulls them out and sets them on the floor between them.

Old correspondence, a list of names, a torn piece of hotel stationery with a number scribbled on it.

Nothing conclusive.

Everything suggestive.

Isla exhales in frustration. "It's like chasing smoke."

"It's like Keir," Callum says.

Isla looks up sharply. "That isn't fair."

Callum's expression stills. "No," he admits. "It isn't. But it's what he did, left evidence without explanation."

Isla presses on because she needs the truth more than she needs comfort. "So don't tell me he didn't think he was allowed. He *allowed* himself to save you."

A muscle jumps in Callum's jaw. He looks away briefly, then back.

"You want the ugliest answer?" he asks quietly.

Isla's chest tightens. "Yes."

Callum swallows. "Because saving me didn't risk destroying you."

Isla goes still.

Callum continues, voice rougher now, like each word costs him. "If he showed up in your life, if he fought Alisa, fought custody, fought the narrative, he knew he'd lose. And he knew you'd be the battlefield."

Isla's eyes sting.

"So he stayed away," she whispers.

Callum nods once. "Knowing him, distance was the only thing he could control."

"That's still cowardice," Isla says, but it comes out smaller now. Wounded.

"Yes," Callum agrees again. "It is."

The honesty hits her harder than defense ever would.

Isla looks down at the papers in her lap, then back up. "And you," she says, voice sharpening, "you still want the castle. Even knowing this."

Callum's breath catches. "I want… what it means."

"That's not an answer," Isla says.

He lifts his gaze, and for a moment, she sees something raw there, fear, maybe, or grief he hasn't named.

"The castle is the only place I've ever belonged," Callum says quietly. "If I lose it, I don't know who I am."

The confession shocks her into silence.

She doesn't soften. Not yet. But something in her shifts, an understanding that Callum's loyalty isn't greed.

It's survival.

The room is silent again, but not hostile. Just full.

Callum exhales, as if he regrets saying too much, and stands. "Keep looking," he says softly. "If we're going to hate the truth, we might as well know it."

Isla rises too.

And this time, when they move through the room, they do it

like partners, side by side, hands occasionally brushing as they reach for the same drawer, the same book, the same corner of the past.

The desk drawer sticks, then slides open. Inside are envelopes stacked neatly. Legal. Financial. Managed.

"He kept everything," Isla murmurs.

"He believed history mattered," Callum replies. "Even when it hurt."

They work in silence again, the air companionable now. At one point, Callum reaches across her to pull down a box from the top shelf. His arm brushes her shoulder, his chest close behind her for a brief second.

Neither of them moves away.

Finally, Callum freezes.

Isla looks up. "What?"

He's holding an envelope she hadn't noticed before. Thicker than the others. Older.

No address.

Just a date.

"This was hidden," Callum says. "Not filed."

Isla's pulse quickens. "That means something."

Callum turns it over slowly. The seal is intact.

"He didn't want this mixed in with the rest," he says.

He looks at her, searching her face. "Are you ready?"

Isla hesitates. Then steps closer.

"Not yet," she says. "But I don't want you to put it down."

Callum nods.

He holds the envelope out, and she places her hand over his, both of them gripping the paper together.

The contact is steady. Intentional.

She looks up at him, surprised by the hope rising inside her, fragile and unwanted and impossible to ignore. This matters. She knows it does. Whatever is sealed inside the envelope could shatter what little certainty she has left, but for the first time, she isn't standing on the edge by herself. They will face it together. The castle settles around them, as if holding its breath.

And Isla knows, absolutely knows—

This envelope is not the end of the story.

It's the beginning of the truth.

CHAPTER 18

They sink down on the bed together, their shoulders touching as Callum rips open the envelope. Isla keeps her hands clasped in her lap, fingers locked so tightly, her knuckles ache. She's afraid that if she reaches for the paperwork, something inside her will split, something she won't be able to stitch back together.

Callum hasn't tried to smooth the moment into something manageable.

Outside, the Scottish afternoon edges toward evening, light thinning behind a veil of clouds. The castle makes its quiet old noises, stone settling, a distant rush through pipes, wind brushing the glass.

Inside Keir's bedroom, time feels suspended.

Isla draws a slow breath and reaches forward. The envelope is heavier than it should be for paper. She pulls out the paperwork, and the pages whisper softly, legal language immediately flattening everything into cold, neat sentences.

She reads the first page aloud without meaning to.

"Irreconcilable differences... marital misconduct... division of assets..."

Her mouth twists. "They always make it sound reasonable."

"That's the point," Callum says, quiet.

She turns the page.

Her eyes catch phrases she's heard her mother say for years, polished into a weapon.

In the interest of stability.

For the child's well-being.

To minimize harm.

Isla exhales sharply. "She uses those words like shields."

Callum leans in slightly. "She believes them."

Isla looks up. "Do you?"

"I believe she believed she was right," he answers.

That distinction lands with a dull thud in Isla's chest. It's easier to hate a villain. It's harder to hate someone who thought she was saving you.

They read on. The custody section is brief, almost dismissive. There's no argument presented on Keir's behalf. The document assumes compliance, as if resistance was never a possibility.

Isla's fingers curl into the paper.

"There," she says, tapping the paragraph. "That clause."

Callum shifts closer and reads it again, his expression sharpening with each word.

No direct or indirect contact.

It doesn't scream. It doesn't threaten in bold letters. It simply *declares*, clinical and absolute, as if love were a dangerous substance and Keir were being ordered to quarantine it.

"No contact," Isla whispers. "Not even letters."

Callum's jaw tightens. "It's absolute."

She flips the page, anger quickening her movements.

"Money," she says, voice rough. "It reduces him to money."

Callum scans. "It reduces him to *risk management*."

The words sting because they're true. This isn't just heartbreak. It's a legal solution to a messy human being.

Isla turns another page, eyes burning.

There it is again: consequences, remedies, and enforcement. The kind of language that feels like handcuffs.

Her laugh is brittle. "They wrote him out of my life and called it protection."

Callum exhales slowly, like he's bracing himself. "They wrote him out legally."

Isla's gaze snaps to his.

"You didn't know about me," she says, knowing she's asked before, but with the legalese they're reading together, she suddenly has doubts.

It isn't a question.

Callum doesn't hesitate. "No. Keir never told me he had a child. Not once. And here's why."

You will not publicly acknowledge your daughter.

The certainty lands like a clean cut, painful but precise. Isla hadn't realized how much she needed to hear that. How much she needed to believe this isn't something Callum carried as a secret too.

"If I'd known," he continues, quieter now, voice roughened by something like anger, "I would've asked why. I would've pushed him. I would have told him he needed to meet his daughter before time ran out."

Isla studies his face for any sign of evasion. Finds none.

"Good," she says, the word barely audible. "I needed to know that."

Callum watches her carefully. "Why?"

Because if he had known, if he had been part of the silence, it would have shattered the one fragile thing Isla has begun to trust here.

"Because if you'd known," she admits, "then I would have lost you too."

Callum stills.

"I wouldn't have let you," he says.

She shakes her head. "Maybe not consciously. But part of me would've wondered if you were another person who agreed I was better loved from a distance."

Callum's mouth tightens. "That wasn't love."

"What was it?" Isla asks.

"Fear," he answers.

She turns back to the papers, because if she looks at him too long, she might let herself believe he means what he says. And belief has always been the most dangerous thing.

They read slowly now.

Not hunting for the next shock. Not skimming. Actually reading.

Callum's eyes move differently than hers; he looks for leverage, intent, what the law allows and forbids. Isla reads for betrayal. For the places her childhood is hidden inside clauses and footnotes.

"This clause," Callum says, pointing lower on the page. "Indirect contact."

Isla leans closer and reads, lips parting.

He can't ask about her through schools. Through venues. Through acquaintances.

"He couldn't even ask if I was okay," Isla whispers.

Callum's gaze hardens. "That's deliberate. That's containment."

The word settles heavy and ugly between them.

Isla can no longer sit beside Callum, she stands, pacing the room as if movement might keep her from collapsing.

"I thought," Isla says finally, voice thin, "that once I knew the truth, it would feel clarifying."

Callum lifts his eyes to hers.

"And?" he asks.

"And instead it feels like someone tilted the world sideways," she answers. "Now nothing lines up."

Callum nods once. Not agreement. Recognition.

"My mother always said he didn't want to be a father," she says, voice sharpening. "That music mattered more."

Callum watches her carefully. "That's not what this says."

Isla stops and turns on him. "Then what does it say?"

"It says he agreed he was a liability," Callum replies. "And she convinced him absence was safer than unpredictability."

Isla's throat tightens. "So he chose exile."

"He chose what he believed would hurt you least," Callum says.

"That's still a choice," Isla snaps.

"Yes," he answers without flinching. "And it cost you."

The honesty hits her harder than defense.

Isla sinks back down on the bed, and flips more pages. There are sections about discretion, reputation, and public exposure. The language has her mother's fingerprints all over it, polished, strategic, brutal in its calm.

"This wasn't only about love," Isla realizes aloud. "It was about image."

Callum nods. "Your mother protected you. And the life she envisioned for you."

Isla swallows, anger turning inward. "She always said she sacrificed everything for me."

"She did," Callum replies gently. "And she also controlled everything."

The duality hurts more than condemnation would. Because Isla can see her mother's fear too, see it as a human thing. Not a villain thing.

Exhaustion washes over her.

"My whole life," she says softly, staring at the papers, "I believed one version of him."

Callum stays silent, giving her room.

"A man who walked away. Who didn't care enough to stay."

Her voice trembles. "I built myself around that. I made it fuel. I became… unstoppable to show him what he was missing."

Her gaze flicks up to Callum's face, then back down. "And now I find out he was legally forbidden from being present."

Callum's voice is steady. "That doesn't erase the damage."

"But it changes the shape of it," Isla whispers.

"Yes."

She flips to the final page.

Signatures.

Her mother's, bold, decisive, unmistakable.

Keir's, smaller than she expects. Controlled. Careful. Almost like someone trying not to tremble.

"He signed it," Isla whispers.

"Under threat," Callum says.

"He could have fought."

"He would have lost," Callum replies. "And he knew the collateral damage would be you."

Isla's chest tightens painfully.

"So he stayed away," she says, the words scraping out of her throat. "And sent money."

"Yes."

"Faithfully."

"Yes."

She laughs softly, hollow. "I never questioned that."

Callum crouches in front of her, bringing himself to eye level. "He did exactly what the agreement allowed. And nothing more."

The truth settles, heavy and final.

"Why didn't my mother tell me?" Isla asks, voice small. "Why didn't Keir come see me after I turned eighteen? She couldn't do anything to him then."

Callum pauses. "Because telling you would've meant admitting she chose control. And how could he explain his absence without making your mother look like a monster?"

Isla closes her eyes. The word she keeps circling lands again.

Managed.

Her childhood suddenly rearranges itself in her mind, memories snapping into new alignment.

The nannies who came and went.

The tutors.

The carefully chosen schools.

The way her mother controlled her schedule down to the minute.

Practice. Lessons. Travel. Performance. A constant message of you have to be a great pianist. What happened to the messages about love and acceptance?

Always moving forward. Never looking back.

"My life was efficient," Isla says slowly. "That's what everyone praised."

Callum doesn't interrupt.

"They said I was disciplined. Focused. Mature for my age." Her mouth twists. "No one ever said I was happy."

Callum's jaw tightens.

"When I cried," Isla continues, voice roughening, "my mother told me feelings were distractions. That I was lucky. Other children had it worse."

The memories of how her mother always made her believe he didn't want her created an ache in her chest. Now it was too late. "And I believed her. Because I didn't know what else to believe."

Callum exhales, slow and controlled. "She gave you consistency."

"Yes," Isla agrees. "And took away choice."

The words hang between them.

She lifts the page again; she has read it three times now, but she needs to see it with her eyes because her heart refuses to accept it.

"When I was eight," Isla says suddenly, "I asked her why my father never came to my recitals."

Callum looks up.

"She told me he was busy," Isla continues. "That his music mattered more than mine. That I shouldn't expect him to show up when he had already chosen his life."

Her voice wavers. "I remember standing backstage that night, listening for applause from a man that never came."

Callum's fists clench at his sides.

"And now," Isla says, tapping the no-contact clause, "I find out he wasn't allowed to come. Not even to stand in the back."

She laughs again, sharp and broken. "I spent my whole life resenting a ghost who wasn't permitted to exist."

Callum steps closer, his presence solid at her side.

"This doesn't absolve him," Isla says quickly, as if daring the thought. "He still signed it. He still chose distance."

"No," Callum agrees. "It doesn't absolve him."

She turns on him. "But it explains why he stayed away."

"Yes."

"And it explains why my mother never told me." Her voice drops. "Because the truth would have cracked the image she built. It explains why she wants me to come home before I learned the truth."

Callum nods.

"She needed you to believe he chose to stay away," he says. "Because that made her the protector."

Isla's breath shudders. "She needed me loyal."

"She needed you safe," Callum corrects gently. "The problem is she defined safety as control."

"So my father removed himself because he thought he was poison," she says. "And my mother removed him because she thought she knew better. And I was never given the choice of seeing him."

Callum's voice is low. "Both of them made choices out of fear."

"And I paid for it," Isla whispers.

Silence presses in again, heavy with understanding rather than shock.

Callum reaches for the papers, gathering them carefully, aligning the edges as if order might help. It's a small action, but it feels intimate, like he's trying to hold the pieces together for her.

"He complied because he didn't believe he deserved you," Callum says. "And she enforced it because she didn't trust him to be restrained and not the rock-n-roll star."

"Look, an envelope addressed to you," he says as it slips from between the pages.

Her heart cracks for just a moment. "Not tonight. I can't take any more. Let's save that for tomorrow."

Isla closes her eyes.

"That might be the cruelest part," she says. "I believe they both loved me. And they both hurt me anyway."

Callum looks at her, something fierce and protective flickering across his expression.

"You deserved better than fear-based love," he says.

The words strike her harder than anger ever could.

For a moment, Isla can't breathe. She has spent her life excelling, achieving, mastering, controlling every space she entered, except the one where love lived. There, she learned to be careful. Restrained. Managed.

She stands abruptly, pacing again, energy coiling tightly inside her chest.

"I don't know who I am without all of that," she admits. "Without the schedule. Without the expectations. Without being the girl who never caused trouble."

Callum watches her. "You're the woman standing here now, and you've been causing your mother some trouble."

She scoffs weakly. "That woman feels like she's coming apart."

"Sometimes that's the only way to find out what's real," he replies.

Isla stops in front of him. "And what if I choose wrong?" she asks, voice trembling.

Callum meets her gaze steadily. "Then you choose again."

The simplicity devastates her.

"All my life," Isla says, "love has meant rules. Distance. Sacrifice disguised as responsibility."

Callum's voice is quiet but sure. "It doesn't have to."

She steps closer, heart pounding.

"What if I don't know how to do it any other way?"

"Then let someone stay," he says. "Not to fix it. Just to be there."

Something inside her cracks open.

Isla lifts her hand, hesitates, then rests it against his chest. His heart beats steadily beneath her palm, real, present, unguarded.

"I don't want to be alone tonight," she says, and this time she doesn't try to disguise the need.

Callum's breath catches. "Tell me to stay."

"Stay," she whispers. "But not here. My bedroom."

His hands slide to her waist, firm and grounding, and the kiss is slow, deliberate, nothing taken, everything offered. It's a kiss that says *I'm here* without demanding she be anything other than what she is right now: furious, grieving, and undone.

Isla clings to him, not because she's weak, but because she's finally letting herself want. Because for the first time in her life, her body has been awakened. While Callum may still be her enemy, she wants him like she's never wanted a man before.

Tonight, she needs to feel his arms around her, holding her, reassuring her that everything will be all right.

When they part, their foreheads rest together, breath mingling.

"This doesn't fix anything," she whispers.

"No," Callum agrees. "But it means you don't face it alone."

She closes her eyes, letting the truth settle in her bones.

Presence.

Not protection.

Not control.

Presence.

Isla takes his hand and leads him from Keir's bedroom. The castle is quiet around them as if listening.

But tonight, Isla chooses what neither of her parents chose for her.

The envelope addressed to her remains on the bed, waiting like a verdict.

She chooses not to be alone.

CHAPTER 19

Callum has slept in a lot of rooms in this castle.

None of them feels like this one.

Isla's bedroom is large, but it doesn't feel imposing. The stone walls soften beneath lamplight, shadows gathering gently in the corners instead of looming. There are no Keir trophies here. No evidence of conquest or legacy. Just signs of a life half-lived elsewhere, an overnight bag, sheet music stacked on the desk, a sweater draped over the back of a chair like she dropped it without thinking.

She didn't create this space.

She's inhabiting it.

Callum stands just inside the door while Isla crosses the room, her movements slow, deliberate, as if she's afraid that if she moves too quickly, the moment will fracture. She sets the divorce papers carefully on the desk, aligning the edges, a familiar gesture now.

Control.

Even here.

Even now.

She turns to him, her face unreadable.

"This doesn't mean I'm not angry," she says.

Callum nods. "I'd be worried if you weren't."

Her mouth twitches, something like relief flickering across her face.

"And it doesn't mean I've forgiven anyone," she adds.

"I wouldn't ask you to," he replies.

She studies him for a long moment, as if weighing something she hasn't yet put into words.

"I don't want to be handled tonight," Isla says quietly. "I don't want to be managed. Or rescued. Or fixed. I just need to feel something besides the hurt that fills me."

The words hit him square in the chest.

"I can do that," Callum says. "But you need to know, if I stay, I stay because you chose me. Not because you're hurt."

Her eyes shine, but she doesn't look away. "You're like a tourniquet to stop the bleeding."

"I know."

"And I'm choosing you anyway."

Something inside him loosens. Something dangerous. All she wants is sex, but a part of him wants so much more.

Callum crosses the room slowly, giving her time to step back if she wants to. She doesn't. She stands her ground, chin lifted, shoulders squared, not defensive, just honest.

He stops in front of her, close enough to feel her warmth.

"This is the part where I should say we can wait," he admits.

She exhales shakily. "And this is the part where I tell you I don't want to."

He nods once. "All right."

He lifts his hand, pauses, and waits.

Isla answers by placing her palm over his wrist, guiding his hand to her waist. Her touch is steady, intentional. Consent made visible.

Callum's breath leaves him slowly. For days, he's dreamed of them together. Naked and willing and tangled in each other's arms.

His mouth descends, and he can't help himself. "Last chance to say no."

"Shut up and fuck me," she whispers.

Desire riddles him like bullet holes, and he kisses her like he never intends to leave. Which is what he's been thinking of. They're both damaged, and they could heal one another.

Her lips part beneath his, and she leans into him, not collapsing, not clinging, meeting him halfway. When his arms come around her, she exhales against his mouth, a sound that goes straight through him.

God.

He has wanted her since the first day he saw her, but this, this isn't want.

This is something deeper. Something that scares him.

He breaks the kiss first, forehead resting against hers, breathing her in.

"Tell me if you want me to stop," he murmurs again.

She shakes her head. "Tell me if you plan to leave."

The question cuts.

"I won't," he says immediately. Then, more carefully, "Not tonight. Not like this."

How can he promise her anything when his own life is in such turmoil?

She nods, accepting the honesty.

They move together toward the bed, not in a rush, not avoiding the moment either. Isla sits on the edge first, hands braced beside her, watching him like she's memorizing this version of him, unguarded, stripped of roles.

Callum kneels in front of her without thinking.

The position feels right. Intentional.

He rests his hands on her knees, grounding himself there, anchoring the moment.

"You should know," he says quietly, "I'm terrified."

Her brows lift. "Of me?"

"No," he answers. "Of being another man who takes something from you and leaves you carrying the weight alone."

Isla's throat works. "Then don't take," she says. "Give."

The word settles into him like a vow, and he moans at the significance.

He lifts his mouth to hers and kisses her again, slower this time, reverent. The world narrows to the warmth of her mouth, the way her fingers curl into his shirt as if holding him in place.

When he finally pulls back, her eyes are dark, bright with emotion she isn't trying to hide.

"Callum," she whispers, like his name is something fragile.

Leaning down to him, she meets him halfway. It is a kiss of desperation and longing, and it takes Callum completely by surprise. Her mouth covers his, moving over his lips, seeking comfort in an age-old connection. And Callum is more than happy to return her kiss, eager, in fact, to soothe and remind her she is still alive.

She moans, the sound encouraging him. Her hands reach beneath his sweater, and she lets her fingernails gently rake his skin. Their lips break apart, and he yanks his sweater over his head as Isla undoes the buttons on her blouse and removes it, leaving only her bra.

Still kneeling before her, he leans over and kisses the tops of her breasts that spill forth. His tongue trails over her smooth skin, and she leans back, giving him access to her throat. Eagerly, he takes her cue and kisses his way across her chest and up her throat, lingering at her ear. He wants to make her feel good. He wants to comfort her and make the demons from the day disappear. He wants to remove all thoughts and envelop her in sensual pleasure.

She pushes him back and stands. Slowly, she slides down the zipper of her jeans and steps out of them, leaving them on the floor. She stands before him, beautiful in her panties and bra.

"God, Isla, you're stunning," he says, reaching for her.

She takes his hand and pulls him up until he's standing, and then she unbuttons his jeans and slides them down his legs.

At first, Callum is a little surprised by the way she takes control. Isla didn't seem like the type to want to lead, but then he realizes that tonight she needs to be in control of something in her life. Taking the lead in their lovemaking is the only thing she has after learning the truth of why her father never came to see her.

He doesn't mind. He's wanted to get her in bed since that first kiss and had been impatiently waiting, knowing instinctively that this woman would somehow fill that empty part of him and hoping he did the same for her.

Grabbing her, he twists her up against the wall and presses his body into hers, letting her feel his erection.

"God," she whispers, clinging to him. "I want you so badly."

Urgently, his hands push her bra down, and her breasts are free for his taking. His mouth wraps around her nipple, and he suckles until she moans.

Her eyes darken with desire, and her breathing is quick and heavy.

"Take me to bed," she gasps. "I need you."

"Gladly," he says and leads her to the bed, where he lies beside her.

His mouth hungrily seeks hers while he runs his hands over her body. He's dreamed of this moment, and now here she is naked in bed with him.

She wraps her fingers around his shaft, and he moans as she strokes him, the pleasure increasing. He doesn't want her to stop, but tonight is all about giving her pleasure. His fingers find her center and caress her as she gasps and writhes upon the bed. She needs this moment as much as he needs her.

His lips taste her skin as he drinks in her beauty, and soon he feels her body tense and shudder beneath his fingers.

"Callum," she cries, reaching her release, and he smiles, knowing he's made her forget for the moment. Made her forget her lousy parenting. Made her forget not knowing her father.

"Oh, my," she said, her breathing rapid and shallow. "Oh, my."

"I love the way you come," he whispers against her mouth, wanting her to feel cherished.

She grins and kisses him before he releases her and finds the condom he'd laid out. Quickly, he rips open the foil packet and stretches the condom over his penis.

Isla crawls on top of him and straddles him. This woman needs to feel in control, and for now, he'll gladly let her. Tonight, he's consoled her, he's made her feel good, and now it's his turn to sink into her body and find his release.

All he wants is to take care of her for the rest of his days, and that thought shocks him. They are still enemies, but they're also now lovers, and he doesn't know what will happen, but for now, this is enough.

After everything she'd endured tonight, having Isla come to him felt like being chosen, not as a refuge from the world, but as shelter within it. When she is with him, the castle, the papers, the ghosts of the past can't touch them. For the first time in years, he feels something steady take hold inside his chest.

Safety.

Care.

Things he'd learned not to expect with his own family. Only from Keir, and now he is gone.

She moves over him, and the way she fit, perfectly, intimately, draws a sharp breath from his lungs. It is like they are made for each other, and he's never experienced that before.

Her reactions, the soft sound she made, tells him how close she already is, how deeply emotion and sensation are tangled for her. It only makes him want to be careful. To be present. To give her everything. And yet the castle remains between them.

She moves with intention, her body answering something deeper than desire. He watches her face as she rides him, the emotion there unmistakable, open, unguarded, fierce. His hands come to her breasts, grounding himself in the reality of her, the heat, the connection.

"Isla," he says, her name leaving him like a truth he can no longer keep inside.

She looks down at him, eyes bright and alive, holding his gaze as if anchoring them together. The moment feels suspended, unreal, like they are leaving the world behind.

He feels it build, the tension coiling tight, knows he's close and doesn't want to pull away from her, not now, not when she is right there with him. When his orgasm finally overtakes him, the release is overwhelming, and the way she follows, calling his name, clinging to him, undoes him completely.

He holds her through it, through the final shuddering moments, until her body finally gives in and she collapses against him, boneless and spent.

For a long time, neither of them move.

Stunned, he holds onto her, knowing that something has just happened between them that is both satisfying and terrifying at the same time.

When he finally shifts, careful not to jostle her, he rolls her gently onto her side and pulls her back against him, fitting himself to her in a way that feels instinctive. Protective. Right.

They lie there together, breathing slowing, hearts finding their rhythm again.

"Isla," he murmurs against her ear. "That was… incredible."

She smiles, soft and satisfied. "You weren't too bad yourself."

Callum closes his eyes, holding her a little closer, knowing with absolute certainty that this, *this,* isn't something he would ever walk away from. He only hopes she feels the same way.

CHAPTER 20

Isla wakes slowly, drifting up through layers of warmth and quiet.

For a few disoriented seconds, she doesn't remember where she is, only that she feels... held. Not physically, not quite, but contained in a way she hasn't felt in years. Safe. Unrushed.

Then memory returns in fragments.

Stone walls.

Lamplight.

Callum's voice, low and steady.

The way he stayed.

She opens her eyes.

Morning light spills across the room, pale and soft, catching in the folds of the curtains and warming the gray stone until it glows. The castle looks different in daylight, less imposing, less haunted. Almost gentle.

Callum is still asleep beside her, one arm thrown loosely across the pillow where her shoulder rests. His face is relaxed, unguarded in a way she hasn't seen before. Without the tension he usually carries, he looks younger. Vulnerable.

Human.

Her heart beats a little faster staring at him. The last time she'd slept with a man was in college, before her first tour. But this feels different. Right in a way, she hadn't anticipated. She remembers the first time she saw him, the way grief had left him stricken.

And then at the funeral, wearing a kilt. The full regalia. He'd been so damn handsome, and yet she'd been filled with anger. Anger that he had gotten to live with her father, and she never had.

But now, he is a rock, strength when she feels like giving up, comfort, and so damn sexy it's all she could do not to pull him into her arms and make love to him once again.

Last night, they had made love way into the morning and only given up when they were both exhausted and out of condoms. And yet, she wants him again.

Staring at him, she studies him quietly, afraid to move too quickly and break whatever fragile magic has settled between them.

Last night wasn't an escape. Last night, he'd driven the demons from her that seemed to reside in her soul.

That's what surprises her most. Now, at least, she has some understanding of why her father never appeared. Now at least, she can begin the healing process.

She'd half-expected to wake with regret or panic or the familiar instinct to armor herself again. Instead, she feels calm. Grounded. As if something that's been clenched inside her for years has finally loosened.

She slips carefully out of bed, pulling on a sweater and crossing to the window. Emerald grass and tall trees stretch out below, green and damp with morning dew. Somewhere in the distance, a bird calls. Life is going on.

For the first time since she arrived, the castle doesn't feel like a battlefield.

It feels like a home.

She hears movement behind her.

Callum's voice is rough with sleep. "You disappeared."

"I'm right here," she says softly.

He sits up, hair rumpled, blinking against the light. When his eyes find her, something gentle settles in his expression, relief, maybe. Or something closer to joy.

"Morning," he says.

She smiles. "Morning."

There's no awkwardness. No scramble for distance or explanation. Just the quiet acknowledgment of what they shared.

Callum swings his legs over the side of the bed. "How are you?"

She considers the question honestly. "Better than I expected."

He nods. "Me too."

Gently, he presses his lips to hers. "You wore me out, woman."

She giggles and realizes that's a sound she hasn't made in years.

"Me too," she says gently.

They dress without ceremony, brushing past each other easily, the intimacy lingering in small, ordinary gestures. When they step into the corridor together, Isla realizes she's humming under her breath.

Callum notices.

"Happy?" he asks.

She pauses, surprised by the word. Then nods. "Yes."

It feels almost rebellious to admit it.

They don't talk about the papers. Or the envelope. Or what comes next.

Instead, Callum takes her hand and leads her down a narrow corridor and through a door to the music room.

Sunlight pours in through tall windows, illuminating the grand piano that dominates the space. Isla stops short, breath catching.

"I forgot how beautiful this room is," she murmurs.

Callum watches her, something like pride flickering across his face. "Keir loved it. Said music needed space to breathe."

"I want to play along with you," he says softly.

She crosses to the piano, running her fingers lightly over the keys. The instrument feels alive beneath her touch, resonant and ready.

"What do you play in the mornings?" Callum asks.

"Whatever needs to come out," she replies.

He disappears for a moment and returns with a guitar, well-worn, familiar. He settles into a chair near the piano, watching her with quiet anticipation.

"Show me," he says. "You lead."

Isla sits, a timid smile crossing her face.

She doesn't think. She just plays.

The melody is simple at first, tentative, like a question asked softly. Then it grows, layering emotion without effort. Not grief this time. Not fury.

Hope.

Callum joins her after a few bars, his guitar threading through her music like it belongs there. They don't discuss key or tempo. They don't need to.

They listen.

They follow. Their music joins them in ways only their bodies could before.

The music swells and ebbs, a conversation without words. Isla laughs once when Callum shifts unexpectedly, catching her off guard with a playful riff.

"Show-off," she accuses.

He grins. "You started it."

They play for a long time, long enough that the world outside fades entirely. When they finally stop, the silence feels full rather than empty.

Isla leans back on the bench, breathless. "That was…"

"Right," Callum finishes.

She nods. "Yes."

They sit together, shoulder to shoulder, basking in the after-glow of sound.

For a moment, Isla lets herself imagine it, mornings like this. Music instead of conflict. Partnership instead of inheritance.

Then her mind drifts, unbidden, to Keir's bedroom.

The single envelope resting on his bed. The one with her name on it.

Callum notices the shift immediately.

"Not yet," he says gently.

She looks at him, grateful. "Thank you."

He reaches for her hand, squeezing once. "We'll open the letter together."

The promise steadies her.

For now, she lets herself lean into the moment, the warmth of the room, the quiet joy, the man beside her who chose to stay.

Just for this morning, she allows herself to be happy.

"I think I'm hungry," she says. "My body needs energy."

A grin spreads across his face. "I'll call Martha to tell her we're ready for breakfast as soon as we shower together."

A giggle escapes her. "Don't tell her we're showering together."

"Oh, I'm sure the entire staff knows what went on in your bedroom last night. We were kind of noisy."

"We were great together," she says.

"We are," he says and gently kisses her.

CHAPTER 21

The walk to Keir's bedroom feels longer than it should.

Callum has lived in this castle long enough to know every shortcut, every stair that creaks, every corridor where sound carries. None of that matters now. The distance stretches anyway, elastic and resistant, as if the house itself is trying to slow them down.

Behind them is breakfast, unfinished coffee, crumbs left on plates, the echo of laughter that had surprised Callum with its ease. Behind them is music, shared without effort, notes folding into one another like they had always been meant to meet.

A shower filled with lingering touches, soft kisses and promises of time later spent in the bedroom.

Ahead of them is a letter. A letter that he fears. Isla has suffered enough heartache. If he could, he would keep this from her, and yet he knows that whatever is inside that letter could also help her heal.

Callum watches Isla as she walks beside him. Her posture is different. Not guarded exactly, but braced. As if she's learned that joy comes with a cost and she's already preparing to pay it.

He hates that he recognizes it.

Keir's bedroom waits at the end of the hall, the door ajar. Light spills across the threshold, softening the sharp lines of the stone floor. The room itself is neat, restrained. Keir had never been a man who let chaos linger in his personal space. Chaos belonged in music, not in the places where he slept.

The envelope sits on the bed, untouched since they last stood here.

White. Ordinary. Heavy.

Isla stops just inside the room.

"This is it," she says.

Callum nods. "We don't have to rush."

She lets out a breath that sounds suspiciously like a laugh. "If I don't do it now, I won't do it at all. I'd like to put this behind me."

She crosses the room and picks up the envelope. Her fingers tighten around it, then loosen again, like she's testing how much pressure it can take.

"I don't want to read it," she says suddenly.

Callum turns toward her. "All right."

"I want you to," she continues. "I need to hear it. I don't think I can… absorb it if it's my voice."

Callum hesitates. He understands the request instinctively and the danger of it.

"If I read it," he says carefully, "you need to know I won't soften it."

She meets his gaze. "Don't."

He takes the envelope from her. The paper is cool beneath his fingers. He breaks the seal slowly, deliberately, as if that might somehow blunt what's coming.

Keir's handwriting fills the page.

Callum recognizes it immediately. Tight, slanted, precise. The handwriting of a man who rewrote every sentence twice before allowing it to exist.

He clears his throat.

Isla,

If you're reading this, then I didn't make it back. I always believed I would have more time.

Isla's breath hitches. Callum forces himself to continue.

I've written and destroyed this letter more times than I can count. Every version felt inadequate. None of them explained why I stayed away in a way that felt honest enough.

Callum's chest tightens.

I want you to know first and foremost that I wanted to come see you. Not once. Not occasionally. All the time.

Isla turns away, pressing her hand flat against the window.

I followed your career the only way I was allowed. Reviews. Recordings. Programs I wasn't supposed to have. I knew when you debuted in Vienna. I knew when you changed your repertoire. I knew when critics finally started using the word "fearless."

Callum's voice wavers despite his effort.

You are extraordinary. I don't say that because you're brilliant, though you are, but because you built yourself without any of the support you deserved. You found your voice without anyone guiding your hands.

Silence presses thickly around them.

When you turned eighteen, I told your mother I was coming. I believed adulthood changed the rules. She told me it didn't.

Callum glances up briefly. Isla hasn't moved.

She told me she had photographs she would release to the press if I showed up. Pictures from my worst years. Pictures I was never proud of. She said she would make sure the world saw exactly who I was.

Isla lets out a sharp, incredulous laugh.

I should have come anyway. I know that now. I tell myself I was protecting you, but the truth is I was afraid. Afraid I'd damage your life. Afraid you'd see me clearly and regret knowing me.

Callum swallows hard.

I imagine playing music with you more times than I can count. You at the piano. Me trying not to embarrass myself. I imagined you rolling your eyes when I missed a beat.

Isla squeezes her eyes shut.

I told myself someday. I told myself I would earn the right.

Callum lowers the letter slightly, breath unsteady, then forces himself to finish.

If I'm gone, then I ran out of time. That is on me. I am so sorry I didn't stand up to your mother. I am so sorry I chose absence when you deserved presence. I loved you from a distance because I didn't know how to do it any other way.

The room feels hollow when he finishes.

Callum lowers the letter.

Isla turns slowly.

Her expression isn't grief.

It's fury.

"So he knew," she says flatly. "He knew, and he still didn't come."

Callum takes a breath. "Isla—"

"He knew she was threatening him," she continues, voice rising. "He knew she was controlling everything, and he stayed away anyway."

"He was terrified," Callum says, unable to stop himself. "Of hurting you. Of ruining you."

"And instead he abandoned me," Isla snaps.

"He didn't abandon you," Callum says.

Her eyes flash. "That's what everyone keeps telling me."

"Because it's true," he replies, immediately wishing he'd chosen different words.

She steps closer, anger radiating. "It's convenient. It makes his silence noble."

"That's not what I mean."

"It's exactly what you mean," she says. "You're defending him."

Callum holds her gaze. "Yes."

All the hurt and anger she'd held onto since she was a child seems to bubble to the surface.

"He should have come," Isla says. "He should have chosen me."

Callum's voice is low. "He thought choosing you meant staying away."

"That was wrong," she fires back.

"Yes," Callum agrees. "It was."

"Then why are you defending him?"

"Because I knew him," Callum says. "And I know what fear does to men who already believe they're dangerous."

Her voice cracks. "And what about what it did to me?"

The question guts him.

She turns away, pacing the room, hands fisted.

"He watched my life from afar," she says. "He read about me instead of showing up. He loved me like a stranger."

Callum watches her, heart pounding. "He loved you the only way he thought he was allowed."

"That's not enough," Isla says. "It was never enough."

She faces him again.

"Stop turning him into a tragic figure," she demands. "He was my father."

Callum exhales slowly. "And he was a man who believed the damage he could cause outweighed the good he might bring."

She shakes her head. "That's cowardice."

"Sometimes," Callum says, "it's fear masquerading as mercy."

The room tightens around them.

"This changes how I see you," Isla says suddenly.

Callum's chest tightens. "How?"

"You defend him," she says. "You see his choice as a sacrifice. I see it as abandonment."

He nods slowly. "Both can be true."

"I don't know how to live with that," she says.

The letter crumples slightly in his hand.

Isla turns and walks out of the room. Callum stands there, not knowing what to do.

The truth has done what it always does.

It hasn't healed them.

It's split them, just enough to hurt. Their fragile beginning seems to be unraveling, and that frightens him.

CHAPTER 22

Callum doesn't go after her right away.

The door closes somewhere down the corridor, the sound swallowed by stone and distance, and he stands there in Keir's bedroom with the letter still in his hand, the words blurring on the page. He tells himself she needs space. That chasing her now will only make things worse. That if he gives her time, they'll find their way back to each other once the initial shock settles.

He tells himself a lot of things.

The truth is simpler and harder to face.

He doesn't know what to say that won't make this worse.

The letter lies open on the bed, the paper creased where Isla's fingers tightened, where his own grip faltered. Keir's handwriting stares up at him, controlled, deliberate, written by a man who believed that if he chose his words carefully enough, he could manage the damage.

Callum folds the letter slowly and places it back into the envelope, not sealing it. Nothing about this feels finished. He sets it on the desk, straightening it as if order might bring clarity.

It doesn't.

The castle feels different now. It did last night too, but then it was softened by warmth, shared music, shared breath, the sense that for once something good wasn't about to be taken away.

Now it feels watchful.

Callum leaves the room and moves through the corridors without direction at first, following instinct more than thought. He hears voices somewhere below, staff going about their day, unaware that something fundamental has just shifted.

He finds Isla in the music room.

She's sitting at the piano bench, hands resting flat on the closed lid, not playing. Her shoulders are tight, her spine rigid, like she's holding herself together through force of will alone.

Callum stops just inside the doorway.

For a long moment, he says nothing. He watches her breathe, the slow rise and fall of her shoulders, the stillness that feels anything but calm.

"You always run when you're overwhelmed," he says quietly.

Isla doesn't turn around. "And you always stand still and call it patience."

The words land clean and sharp.

Callum steps into the room, careful not to crowd her. "I didn't want to chase you."

Her laugh is humorless. "I didn't want to be chased."

They sit with that truth for a beat, two instincts colliding without canceling each other out.

Callum shifts closer, stopping a few feet away. "I didn't want to make you feel trapped."

She turns then, slow and deliberate, arms crossing over her chest like she's holding herself together.

"I can't do this," Isla says.

The finality in her voice makes his chest tighten. "Do what?"

"This," she snaps, gesturing between them. "This pattern."

"We don't have a pattern," Callum replies, though even as he says it, doubt flickers.

"Yes, we do," Isla says. "I let myself feel something good, and then it's immediately reframed into something I have to justify or forgive."

Callum takes a breath. "You can feel good things without punishment."

She tilts her head, studying him. "Can I?"

She stands abruptly and begins to pace, one step, then another, like motion is the only thing keeping her upright.

"Last night," Isla says, voice tight, "I let myself be open. I let myself want someone without bracing for loss."

Callum's throat tightens. He felt it too, the choice, the trust, the way she let herself be held without armor.

"And today," she continues, "we open a letter, and it's the same story again. Men leaving. Women controlling. Love turned into a justification."

"I'm not asking you to forgive him," Callum says.

"You keep defending him," she fires back.

"I keep insisting he was human," Callum replies. "And afraid. He made mistakes. We all make mistakes."

"And I keep insisting that fear doesn't excuse disappearing," Isla snaps. "Do you hear me? He disappeared."

Callum exhales slowly. "He thought he was protecting you."

"That's what I keep hearing," she says bitterly. "Because it's convenient."

The word hangs heavy between them.

"It turns his absence into something noble," Isla continues. "Instead of a choice he made."

Callum opens his mouth to argue and then closes it again.

Because she's not wrong.

The realization settles heavily in his chest, tangled with something else he doesn't want to name yet.

He has the disorienting sense that he's standing at the edge of something he doesn't know how to survive losing.

Not Isla.

The certainty.

The castle has always been a constant. Even before he understood what it meant, before he knew its history or the weight of its name, it had been there, walls that didn't move, a roof that didn't vanish, a place that did not ask him to earn his right to exist within it.

After his father died, everything else became conditional. His mother's love, suddenly rationed. Her patience exhausted. Her attention redirected. Her love redirected to another man.

The castle never asked him to adapt.

It held him while he was angry. While he was silent. While he was closed off, difficult, and impossible.

Now Isla stands before him, asking him to choose.

The request terrifies him more than he wants to admit.

Not because he doesn't love her.

But because love has never been the thing that kept him safe.

Stone did.

Routine did.

Staying put did.

Isla represents movement. Change. Risk. A future that doesn't come with instructions.

He understands, suddenly, why Keir stayed away.

Not because Keir didn't love her.

But because loving someone that much makes you realize how much damage you're capable of causing. For the hurt that loving can cause and when the love ends, you get sent to a boys' school.

Callum hates himself for understanding it.

"Do you know what scares me the most?" Isla asks quietly, pulling him back.

He shakes his head.

She looks at him then, really looks at him, as if memorizing something she doesn't trust herself to keep.

"It's not that you love this place," she says. "It's that it loves you back."

He frowns. "What does that mean?"

"It means the castle doesn't ask anything of you," Isla replies. "It doesn't need reassurance or compromise or honesty. It doesn't get angry when you hesitate."

Callum stiffens. "You think I'm choosing the castle because it's easier."

"I think you're choosing it because it's safe," she says gently. "And I don't blame you for that."

The gentleness devastates him more than anger would have.

"I grew up with love that came with rules," Isla continues. "With expectations I didn't get to negotiate. My mother decided what was best for me and called it protection. My father stayed away and called it mercy. The castle shows neither."

Her voice tightens. "Both of them took something from me and told themselves they were being kind."

Callum's chest aches.

"I can't live inside that again," she says. "I can't love someone who needs me to soften myself so they don't have to decide."

"That's not what I'm asking," he says hoarsely.

"But it's what you're doing," Isla replies. "Every time you hesitate."

She steps closer now, close enough that he can feel the pull of her.

"I love you," she says quietly. "But I will not become negotiable. We support one another, or we walk away."

Silence stretches between them, thick and charged.

"And I won't stay here within these stone walls," Isla finishes softly.

Callum's heart pounds.

"Say you choose me," Isla says, voice trembling. "Say it without flinching."

He wants to.

God, he wants to.

But the castle is not just stone to him. It is the place that kept him when no one else did. The only thing that never left.

His silence lasts a heartbeat.

Two.

Isla's face stills, all emotion draining into something quiet and devastating.

"There it is," she whispers. "You choose the castle over me."

"I love you," Callum says, the words tearing out of him.

Isla closes her eyes. When she opens them, she looks wrecked.

"I love you too," she says. "That's the problem."

She turns toward the door, then pauses.

"I don't regret last night," Isla says quietly. "I don't regret choosing you."

Callum swallows hard. "Isla—"

She looks back at him, eyes shining. "No, it's more than that. It's a place that teaches me to disappear."

And then she leaves.

Callum follows her only as far as the doorway.

He watches her walk down the corridor, her back straight, steps steady, already carrying the weight of a decision he doesn't yet understand.

The castle swallows her, and Callum understands too late what she sees when she looks at it. It belonged to her father, and her father left her. In her mind, the walls and the silence are the same thing, both reminders of how love can vanish without warning.

Callum stands there long after she's gone, the echo of her words reverberating through him.

I won't stay somewhere that teaches me to disappear.

CHAPTER 23

*I*sla doesn't sleep.

She lies awake in the dark, staring at the ceiling as the castle settles around her, the old stones creaking and sighing like something alive. The sounds are constant once she starts listening: the low groan of beams adjusting to the cold, the whisper of air moving through corridors never meant to be sealed, the faint echo of footsteps that aren't there.

The castle has never been quiet.

It breathes. It remembers.

She rolls onto her side and closes her eyes, but memory crowds in anyway. Callum's hands. His voice, low and careful when he was trying not to say the wrong thing. The way he looked at her this morning when she laughed without guarding herself.

He does not come to her.

That hurts more than she wants to admit.

She tells herself he's giving her space, that he's doing the respectful thing. That if he came now, everything would fracture completely. She would give in. She would stay. She would tell herself that love is worth any compromise.

And that terrifies her.

She has spent her entire life earning her place in the world. Earning approval. Earning space. Earning the right to exist without apology. She knows how easily love can turn into a negotiation where she is the one making concessions.

She will not do that again.

The decision settles heavily in her chest, not sharp but constant. This is grief, not panic. This is choice, not escape.

She rises before dawn, moving quietly, deliberately. There is no rush. She dresses slowly, pulling on jeans and a sweater, folding each movement into the next like ritual. The suitcase at the foot of the bed waits for her, already packed.

That realization stings.

She crosses the room and sits at the small desk by the window. Outside, the sky is still dark, the horizon just beginning to soften into gray. She takes out a sheet of paper and a pen and stares at the blank page.

Writing has never scared her.

This does.

She presses the pen down and begins, stopping and starting more than once before the words finally come.

Callum,

I'm leaving before this becomes something I can't undo.

That doesn't mean I don't love you. It means I love myself enough not to disappear.

If I stay, I will start doing what I've always done, explaining my pain until it's reasonable, justifying my anger until it's quiet, telling myself that love means understanding why men hesitate instead of asking them to stand.

I don't want to be brave like that anymore.

I love you. I love the way you listen when you don't know what to say. I love the way you stay when things are uncomfortable. I love the way you belong here.

And that's the truth I can't ignore.

This castle chose you long before it ever knew me. It held you when nothing else did. I would never forgive myself if I became the reason you lost it.

I'm leaving it to you. All of it. Not because I'm running, but because I'm choosing what won't break either of us.

Please don't follow me out of guilt or obligation. Only come if you know, without hesitation, that you're choosing me.

I love you. I always will.

—Isla

Her hand trembles as she sets the pen down.

She folds the letter carefully, smoothing the crease as if precision might make this less painful. She places it on the bed where he will find it, then sets the signed legal documents giving him the castle on top. She doesn't look at them again. If she does, she might falter.

She stands there for a long moment, absorbing the finality of it.

This is her black moment, not because she doubts the choice, but because she knows the cost.

She moves through the castle one last time, barefoot now, the stone cool beneath her feet. She pauses in the music room, resting her hand lightly on the piano lid. For a heartbeat, she considers playing something, one final note, one last memory.

She doesn't.

Some things are better left untouched.

Putting her boots on, she hauls her suitcase down the steps, remembering when she arrived.

At the front door, she hesitates.

The castle feels restless, the air shifting as if the walls themselves are aware of her leaving. When she opens the heavy door, a low sound rises through the stone, deep and old, almost a moan. The place seems to resist her, mourning in its own ancient way.

Her throat tightens.

"It's not you," she whispers, absurdly. "It's me."

The words feel thin even as she says them.

She steps outside into the morning, pulling her coat tight as mist curls around her ankles. She does not look back. If she does, she won't keep walking.

As the car pulls away, the castle looms behind her, solid, unmoving, full of history and ghosts.

She presses her forehead to the window, tears finally spilling.

She is leaving the man she loves.

She is leaving the place that feels like grief given form.

She tells herself this is strength. That choosing herself is not abandonment. That love does not always mean staying.

Still, the ache is relentless.

And somewhere beneath the resolve and the sorrow, a single, terrifying thought takes root:

What if love was the one thing she wasn't supposed to walk away from?

The plane lifts off hours later, carrying her back to New York, back to contracts and schedules and a life she understands.

But the castle follows her.

So do thoughts of Callum.

She doesn't know yet which one will matter more.

CHAPTER 24

Callum wakes to light.

Ashen and thin, filtering through the tall windows like it's unsure whether it belongs. The castle always wakes before he does, pipes shifting, stone settling, the distant movement of staff beginning their routines.

This morning, something feels… muted.

Not silent. The castle is never silent.

But subdued. As if it's holding its breath. Waiting to see what happens between him and Isla.

Callum lies still for a moment, staring at the ceiling, letting consciousness return slowly. His body remembers before his mind does, the warmth of another person, the weight of connection, the sense that something had shifted irrevocably the night before.

Isla.

He sits up, rubbing a hand over his face. The bed is rumpled from his sleep. They had slept in her bedroom, and now he feels like he's sleeping in the wrong room.

Still, unease coils low in his gut.

He listens.

No movement in the corridor. No faint sound of a door opening or closing. No distant music drifted through the stone the way it had the morning before. The way it had every morning since she'd been here.

Yesterday morning.

The word *yesterday* feels heavier than it should.

Callum swings his legs over the side of the bed and stands, pulling on a shirt as he crosses the room. He tells himself she went for a walk because she needed air. That she needed distance after everything they'd uncovered.

That she'll come back.

He moves through the castle with measured steps, not rushing, not yet willing to acknowledge what his instincts are already whispering.

The music room is empty. There is no scattered music on the stand.

The piano lid is closed. The bench pushed neatly into place, as if no one had sat there laughing, improvising, sharing something unguarded less than twenty-four hours ago.

The dining room is set, but only for one.

That's when his chest tightens.

Isla isn't careless. She doesn't leave traces unintentionally. She doesn't half-finish things. If she were here, there would be some sign, an interruption, a disruption, a sense of her presence lingering in the air.

There is nothing.

Callum turns back toward the stairs slowly, dread threading deeper with each step. He takes them two at a time, not running, but no longer pretending this is nothing.

When he reaches her bedroom, he stops short.

The room looks…cold and uninviting.

Not lived in.

Not empty in the way a room is when someone simply steps out, but stripped of the small, human disruptions that mark temporary belonging. The sweater she'd tossed over the chair is gone. The book she'd left on the nightstand is gone.

And then he sees it.

The letter.

It rests on the bed, centered with deliberate care, like a period placed at the end of a sentence that had once promised continuation. Beneath it, a neat stack of documents.

Callum's name.

He stands there for a long moment, unable to move.

This is not impulse.

This is intention.

His hand shakes slightly as he picks up the letter. He doesn't sit. He doesn't brace himself. He just opens it and reads.

Once.

Twice.

Each word lands with devastating clarity.

If I stayed, I would disappear.

Callum presses his thumb into the paper, breathing hard. The room feels suddenly too small, the air too thin.

She knew exactly what she was doing.

She loved him enough to leave.

The realization cuts deeper than anger ever could.

His gaze drops to the documents beneath the letter, legal language stark and unyielding. The castle. The land. Everything.

Given to him.

Left behind.

"No," he whispers, the word useless against ink and signature. He wants her, not the castle.

He sinks onto the edge of the bed, the weight of the letter pressing into his chest like a physical thing. The castle creaks softly around him, the sound winding through stone and beam until it settles in his bones.

It feels wrong now.

Too big. Too quiet.

Like a body without a pulse.

He thinks of her laugh in the music room. The way she teased him when he missed a chord. The look in her eyes when she trusted him, really trusted him, to hold something fragile without breaking it.

He'd wanted to be worthy of that.

Instead, he hesitated.

The castle exhales, a low sound rising through the walls, ancient and mournful. Callum feels it echo through him, grief layered on grief, absence piled atop inheritance.

For the first time, the place does not feel like shelter.

It feels like a monument.

He rises slowly and crosses to the window. Fog lingers over the land, damp and gray, the road leading away already empty.

She's gone.

Not in anger.

Not in haste.

But with resolve.

Keir stayed away and called it mercy.

Isla left and called it survival.

And Callum—

Callum stayed.

The truth settles heavy and unavoidable.

He grips the window frame, jaw tightening as something sharp and bright cuts through the devastation.

No.

He will not repeat the same mistake.

Stone does not love you back.

Walls do not choose you.

People do.

And for the first time in his life, Callum understands that what kept him safe once is not what will save him now.

He turns from the window, letter still clenched in his hand, heart pounding with something that finally feels like clarity.

This is not the end.

CHAPTER 25

*I*sla doesn't go home.

That decision is made before the car even pulls away from the airport. Her phone vibrates in her hand, her mother's name lighting up the screen like a summons, and something inside Isla finally… stills.

Not fear.

Clarity.

She answers on the third ring.

"What time do you land?" her mother asks without preamble. "I'll have a car waiting."

Isla closes her eyes briefly. When she opens them, the city is already rushing past the window, sharp and familiar and entirely unchanged.

"I'm not coming home," she says.

Silence crackles on the line.

"What do you mean you're not coming home?" Alisa asks, her tone sharpening. "Isla, you've been gone long enough. We need to talk about your schedule."

"We're going to talk," Isla says. "But not about my schedule."

A pause. Calculated.

"Where are you?" her mother asks.

"Manhattan."

Another pause, longer this time. "You should come home. You're exhausted."

Isla lets out a quiet laugh. "I've never been more awake. Meet me at the hotel. We need to talk."

She hangs up without waiting for permission.

The hotel lobby smells like polished stone and restraint. Neutral. Impersonal. Safe. Isla checks in under her own name, no assistant, no manager, no handler, smoothing the edges.

She barely closes the door to her room when there's a knock.

She opens it to find her mother standing there, impeccably dressed, composed as ever. The woman who taught her how to perform long before she ever touched a piano.

"May I come in?" Alisa asks.

Isla steps aside.

Her mother takes in the room with a quick, appraising glance. "A hotel?"

"I needed space," Isla replies.

"You need rest," Alisa counters. "And to get back on track. How can you practice here?"

Isla closes the door and turns to face her. "I've rented space in a studio."

Her mother's expression is concerned.

"I read the divorce decree."

The words drop like a match.

Alisa stills.

"That's not appropriate reading," her mother says coolly. "Those were private matters between your father and myself."

"It was my life," Isla snaps. "And you made decisions about it without me."

Alisa exhales sharply. "I protected you."

"No," Isla says. "You controlled me."

Her mother's eyes flash. "You were a child. He was into drugs and wild sex parties. Something a child didn't need to be around."

"He changed."

"Oh, don't believe that."

"When I was eighteen," Isla fires back, "my father wanted to see me."

"That's not—"

"I know he told you he was coming," Isla interrupts. "I know you threatened him."

The room tightens.

Her mother shrugged her shoulders and licked her lips.

"You don't know what you're talking about," Alisa says.

"I know you told him you'd release photos," Isla continues, voice steady now, deadly calm. "I know you told him you'd destroy him publicly if he showed up."

Her mother's jaw tightens. "He was dangerous. He would ruin your reputation. He would destroy everything we were working for."

"He was my father."

"He was unstable," Alisa snaps. "He was reckless. He would have dragged you into chaos. No one wants a concert pianist with a drug habit or a father who entices you into rock-n-roll."

"And that was your decision to make?" Isla demands to know, staring at the woman who had made all the decisions regarding her career.

"Yes," Alisa says without hesitation. "Because someone had to. Your job was to be a great pianist. Mine was to make certain that nothing derailed your career. Not your father. Not your education. Not any boy who tried to come around. You had the talent, and I was going to make you a star."

Isla laughs, a sound stripped of humor. "You didn't just keep him away from me. You made sure he stayed away. You're telling me you kept everyone away."

"I did what was necessary," Alisa says. "And it worked."

She'd always known her mother was ambitious, but this felt like a betrayal disguised as determination.

"Worked?" she repeats. "You mean I became exactly what you wanted?"

Alisa lifts her chin. "You became successful."

"I became obedient," Isla says. "There's a difference."

Her mother's expression hardens. "Everything you have is because I managed you. Because I made certain you became a great pianist."

"And everything I lost is because you controlled me," Isla replied.

They stand there, the truth finally unmasked between them.

"You took away my choice," Isla says. "You took away my father. And you told yourself it was because of love? What about the love I had for my father?"

Alisa's voice sharpens. "You would have been destroyed by him."

"No," Isla says quietly. "I was destroyed by not knowing him."

Silence crashes down.

"You don't get to rewrite this," Alisa says finally. "You don't get to undo years of careful planning because you read a document. I've made you who you are."

"I get to stop," Isla replies. "I get to choose now."

Her mother scoffs. "You're emotional. This will pass."

"No," Isla says. "This ends."

She reaches into her bag and pulls out a legal document, setting it on the table between them.

"You're no longer my manager."

Alisa's face goes pale. "Don't be ridiculous."

"I've already contacted my attorney," Isla continues. "And a new representation agency. My contracts are being transferred. I have new staff. A new manager. Everyone you chose has been replaced."

"You're making a mistake," Alisa says sharply. "You don't understand this industry."

"I understand control," Isla says. "And I'm done living under it."

Alisa's composure finally cracks. "After everything I've sacrificed—"

"This isn't about your sacrifice," Isla says. "It's about my life."

Her mother stares at her, stunned.

"You're choosing chaos," Alisa says.

Isla shakes her head. "I'm choosing freedom."

She opens the door.

"I'm not coming home," Isla adds. "When I find a place, I'll have my assistant come and pack up my things."

Alisa looks at her for a long moment, eyes cold, calculating.

"Your father was a drug addict who cheated on me. You're choosing him over me?"

"I'm choosing freedom. I'm choosing truth. I'm choosing to make my own mistakes," she said, feeling certainty in her bones. This is right.

"You'll regret this," she says.

Isla meets her gaze without flinching. "Maybe. But it will be mine alone."

Alisa leaves without another word.

Isla closes the door and leans back against it, heart hammering. Her legs feel unsteady, her breath shallow, but beneath the adrenaline is something unfamiliar and fragile.

Relief.

She crosses the room and sinks onto the bed, staring at the ceiling. Maybe someday she can forgive her. Maybe someday they can make up. But for now, she needs this space to learn to live on her own.

She has confronted the woman who shaped her entire life.

She has cut the final thread of control.

She is alone in a New York hotel room, with no plan, no handler, no safety net.

And for the first time, the fear feels like her own.

She pulls the curtains open and looks out at the city, bright and unyielding.

Somewhere far away, there is a castle waiting.

For now, Isla lets herself sit in the quiet aftermath of choosing herself, heartbroken, furious, and finally free.

She knows her father would have been proud of her today, proud that she finally spoke for herself and for him. And yet, even in the quiet, his music plays in her head, a reminder that pride and grief can exist at the same time.

What would her father have thought of her and Callum? Would he have encouraged it, or warned her away from the man she's fallen in love with?

CHAPTER 26

The castle is too quiet.

Not the normal quiet of early morning, of stone and weather and distance, but the kind that follows a slammed door. The kind that means something has been said that can't be taken back.

Once again, Callum stands in Isla's bedroom with her letter in his hand and the legal papers spread across the bed like a verdict. He has read her words so many times, the ink feels carved into his palm.

If I stayed, I would disappear.

He keeps coming back to that line, not because it hurts the most, though it does, but because it explains everything. It explains why she left without a confrontation, why she didn't give him another chance to hesitate.

Because she learned the hard way that hesitation is its own kind of answer.

He sits on the edge of the bed and thinks about the night they spent together. They only slept together one night, one perfect, impossible night, and still the room feels altered, as if the air remembers and is offended by the return to emptiness.

He should be angry.

He tries to be.

But anger requires a villain, and Callum can't make Isla one. Not when he can trace every step of her decision back to a single moment: the look on her face when she asked him to choose her without flinching.

And he didn't.

It wasn't even a refusal. That would have been cleaner. Easier to forgive.

It was a pause.

A heartbeat of uncertainty.

A single breath where the castle won. When the stones he'd desired overcame his need to choose the woman he loved.

Callum presses the letter to his chest and closes his eyes.

He can still hear her voice from the music room, steady, defiant, quietly breaking.

I won't stay somewhere that teaches me to disappear. Someone who doesn't choose me.

Stone taught her that men vanish. That love is conditional. That control can wear the mask of protection.

And Callum, God help him, had stood there with a lifetime of loyalty to this place lodged in his ribs and had expected her to understand.

He picks up the legal papers, scans the crisp signatures, the formal language. The words are cold, efficient, final. They feel like a transfer of property and a transfer of guilt.

This is what she left him.

A castle.

An inheritance.

A choice he didn't make.

He sets the papers down, hands shaking slightly.

He needs to breathe, but the air in this room tastes like old regrets. He stands and walks to the window. The grounds spread out below, damp and gray, the road leading away already scrubbed clean by distance. There are no tire tracks left. No visible proof she was ever here.

Only the absence.

Callum grips the windowsill. His knuckles whiten.

He has spent most of his life believing that staying was strength.

Stay when it's hard. Stay when people leave. Stay when you're unwanted. Stay because leaving means you're weak. Leaving means you're like everyone else who walked away.

Keir stayed away.

And called it love.

Isla left.

And called it survival.

Callum stayed.

And called it home.

The pattern is so obvious, it makes him feel sick.

He's been furious at Keir before, furious that a man who could write songs that cracked people open could still make choices that ruined lives. Furious that he could be brilliant and selfish in the same breath. Furious that he could care and still fail.

Now Callum understands something he didn't want to.

It's possible to love someone and still choose wrong.

It's possible to believe you're protecting someone when you're really protecting yourself.

The door behind him creaks.

Callum turns, expecting no one, and finds Mrs. Grant, the housekeeper, standing at the threshold. Her gray hair is pinned tight, her expression polite but knowing. In this castle, nothing happens unnoticed for long.

"I knocked," she says, as if that excuses the intrusion.

Callum drags a hand through his hair. "Sorry. I didn't hear."

Her gaze flicks to the bed, to the letter, to the papers. She doesn't comment. But her eyes soften.

"She's gone, then," Mrs. Grant says quietly.

Callum swallows. "Yes."

Mrs. Grant nods once, as if confirming what the castle already told her. "I thought she might."

The bluntness stings. "You thought she'd leave?"

"I thought she'd do what she had to," Mrs. Grant replies. Then, almost gently: "She's got that look about her. The look of a woman who's been told no too many times."

Callum's chest tightens. "I didn't tell her no."

Mrs. Grant's eyes sharpen. "No. You just didn't tell her yes."

The words land hard and clean.

Callum doesn't argue because he can't.

Mrs. Grant steps fully into the room. "What will you do?"

He looks at the papers again, then back at her. His voice is raw. "I don't know."

She studies him. "That's a lie."

Callum flinches.

"Men always say they don't know," she continues, matter-of-fact. "What they mean is they know, but they're afraid of the cost."

Callum's throat works. He hates how easily she sees through him. Maybe everyone sees through him, and he's the last to admit it.

He looks at the castle around him, Keir's room, Keir's handwriting, Keir's shadow in every corner.

The castle has saved him, yes.

It has also trapped him.

Keir used to say the castle was a sanctuary. Callum is beginning to suspect it's also a cage, beautiful, gilded, comfortable enough that you forget there's a door.

Mrs. Grant waits, not impatient, just certain.

Callum sets Isla's letter down carefully on the bed as if it's something fragile. He smooths it once, his hand lingering on the paper, on her name, on the final line.

I love you.

He takes a breath.

"I'm going after her," he says.

The words feel like stepping off a cliff. Terror and relief in the same heartbeat.

Mrs. Grant nods, unsurprised. "Good."

Callum blinks. "Good?"

She gives him a look that could slice stone. "Did you think I'd tell you to sit in this room and mourn while she disappears into her life again?"

His mouth tightens. "She left because she didn't want to disappear."

"Aye," Mrs. Grant says. "And now you'll go and prove she doesn't have to."

Callum's chest aches. "She left me the castle."

Mrs. Grant waves that away with a small flick of her hand. "She left you a test, more like."

Callum stares at her.

"She wants to know what you'll choose," Mrs. Grant says, as if explaining something obvious. "She wants to know whether you'll hold on to stone or go after flesh and blood."

Callum's stomach twists.

Because that's exactly it.

The castle has always been his excuse.

His constant.

His reason to stay put.

If he leaves, he risks everything: legal mess, headlines, responsibility, the gnawing fear that if he steps away, the only home he's ever had will stop being his.

If he stays… he will become exactly what Isla fears.

Another man who explains absence.

Another man who chooses safety and calls it love.

Callum turns away from the bed and walks down the hall to his bedroom. Mrs. Grant follows. He opens his wardrobe and begins to pull clothes out: shirts, jeans, a coat. He packs quickly, not neatly. Function over ritual. His hands move with a strange urgency, as if speed can make up for yesterday.

Mrs. Grant watches him for a moment. "Where will you go?"

"New York," he says, the word foreign in his mouth. "She said she was going there."

Mrs. Grant nods. "And how will you find her in a city that size?"

Callum pauses. The practical question cuts through emotion like cold water.

He exhales and forces his mind to work. Isla's world is schedules, venues, and hotels. She would go to a hotel, not her mother's. She had told him she had concert commitments. And she'd mentioned Long Island, but she said she wasn't going home.

Callum reaches for his phone with fingers that don't quite cooperate.

He scrolls until he finds the number Isla's assistant had called him with to coordinate something with him, before the assistant was replaced by her mother's voice in every decision.

He hesitates. Pride tries to rise.

He crushes it.

This is not the time for pride.

He calls.

It rings.

Once. Twice.

A woman answers, brisk. "This is Kendra."

"This is Callum Fraser," he says. His voice is rough, and he doesn't soften it. "I need to know where Isla is."

A pause. Wariness. "Mr. Fraser—"

"Please," Callum says, and the word surprises him with its nakedness. "Tell me where she is."

Silence stretches.

Then Kendra exhales. "She checked into the Larkwell in Manhattan. Under her name. No press. No entourage. Just her. She's fired everyone but me."

Shocked, Callum closes his eyes in relief so sharp, it hurts. She's cleaning house, getting rid of the parts that hurt. Taking control. "Thank you."

"Is she okay?" Kendra asks quietly, the briskness gone.

Callum swallows. "She's… trying to be."

Another pause. "Do you want me to tell her you're coming?"

"No," Callum says immediately.

Because this can't be managed into safety. It can't be coordinated, smoothed, made convenient.

He needs to show up.

He ends the call and turns back to packing, faster now.

Mrs. Grant steps forward. "What about the castle?"

Callum stares at her. "That's the problem, isn't it?"

"No," she says. "That's the excuse."

He closes his eyes, jaw clenched.

He grabs the legal papers from Isla's bed and shoves them into a folder. He can't leave them scattered. He can't pretend they don't exist. But he can't let them be the anchor that keeps him here.

When he passes Keir's office, he walks to the desk, opens a drawer, and pulls out one of Keir's old guitar picks, little scraps of plastic Keir never threw away, like he believed even the smallest tool mattered if it made music.

Callum holds one in his palm, a ridiculous talisman.

Keir had lived by desire and recklessness.

Callum will do better.

He will live by choice.

He slings his bag over his shoulder, then stops and looks around the room one last time. Keir's room. Keir's castle. Keir's ghost, always there, always watching.

"I'm not repeating you," Callum says quietly, not sure who he's talking to. Keir. Himself. The castle.

Mrs. Grant's gaze softens. "Good."

Callum walks out of the office and down the corridor without looking back. Each step feels like tearing something loose from inside his ribs, but the pain is clean, purposeful.

At the front door, he pauses.

The castle seems to sigh, deep and old, as if it recognizes what's happening.

For years, it has held him.

Now it tries to keep him.

Callum rests his hand against the cold stone beside the doorframe.

"Thank you," he murmurs, surprising himself.

Then, because he finally understands what Isla understood before he did, he adds, "But you're not enough."

He pulls the door open and steps into the morning.

The air bites. The world feels too wide.

And for the first time in his life, that doesn't feel like danger.

It feels like possibility.

Callum walks to the car waiting in the drive. Mrs. Grant already arranged it, of course, because this castle has always been full of people who do the right thing quietly.

He slides into the back seat and gives the driver the address of the nearest airport.

As the car pulls away, he doesn't look back at the castle.

Not because he doesn't love it.

Because he finally knows what love is supposed to do.

It's supposed to move.

It's supposed to show up.

And this time, Callum will.

CHAPTER 27

The hotel room is too quiet.

Isla sits on the edge of the bed, her phone facedown beside her, the city humming far below the windows. New York has always made her feel powerful, anonymous, capable, surrounded by momentum. But today it feels distant, like she's watching her life through glass.

She did the right thing.

She repeats it like a mantra.

She stood up to her mother. She ended the control. She walked away from a place that threatened to swallow her whole. She chose herself.

So why does it feel like she left something unfinished?

Her chest tightens, and she presses her palm there, breathing through it. Love isn't supposed to feel like this, like something you abandon to survive.

All day, she has blocked the thought of Callum from her mind. It's time to forget him, heal from him, and yet her heart is breaking, and tonight, you could add a huge dose of loneliness to that thought.

She misses him. And yet he chose the castle over her. Time to move on. Only her fragile organ is refusing to listen.

In the two days since she arrived in New York, she's cleaned house, met with her new manager, and even spent some time in the studio she rented. But now, it's evening, and she's lonely.

She thinks about her father out on the road without her mother at his side. Was that one of the reasons he'd gotten into trouble and cheated on his wife? Being alone on the road?

A knock sounds at the door.

Isla freezes.

Her first thought is of her mother. Her second is worse.

Hope.

She stands slowly, heart pounding, and crosses the room. She tells herself not to expect anything. Not to read meaning into coincidence. Not to open the door looking for rescue.

She opens it anyway.

Callum stands in the hallway.

No jacket. No castle. No hesitation.

Just him.

For a heartbeat, neither of them speaks.

He looks different, rumpled, travel-worn, eyes bright with something that looks like fear and resolve tangled together. Not the man who hesitated. The man who moved.

Her breath leaves her in a rush.

"You came," she says, the words barely audible.

"Yes," Callum replies. "I did."

The simplicity of it undoes her.

She steps back without thinking, letting him inside. The door clicks shut behind him, sealing them back into the quiet, but now it feels charged, alive.

"I didn't know if you would," Isla admits.

"I didn't know if I deserved to," he says honestly.

They stand there, the space between them heavy with every-thing they didn't say the two nights before.

"I read your letter," Callum continues. "About five times before I stopped shaking."

Isla's throat tightens. "I meant every word."

"I know," he says. "That's why I'm here."

She folds her arms, instinctive armor rising. "You didn't come to convince me to go back."

"No," Callum says immediately. "I came to tell you I was wrong."

The words land cleanly, without defensiveness.

Isla searches his face. "About what?"

"About staying," he says. "About believing that standing still was loyalty. About letting fear masquerade as responsibility."

Her heart stutters.

"I thought the castle was what made me solid," Callum continues. "What kept me from becoming someone who left when things got hard."

"And instead…" Isla prompts softly.

"And instead I almost became exactly that," he finishes. "A man who explains absence instead of correcting it."

Her eyes burn.

"I didn't come here to ask you to come back," he says. "I came to tell you I'm choosing you. No caveats. No conditions."

She swallows. "What about the castle?"

His mouth tilts in a sad smile. "It'll still be there. Stone doesn't vanish when you turn your back on it."

"And you?" she asks quietly.

"I choose you," he says. "Not that big pile of rocks, but you. Your happiness. We may not always agree about your father, but you're the one who matters, not him. Not the castle. Only you."

The honesty breaks something open inside her.

"I was so afraid," Isla admits. "Afraid that if I stayed, I'd disappear. That I'd start making myself smaller just to keep something beautiful."

Callum steps closer, slow and deliberate. "I don't want you smaller. I want you larger than life."

"I know," she whispers. "I just needed to know you wouldn't need me to be smaller."

He stops a breath away from her.

"I don't want a woman who stays because it's safer," Callum says. "I want a woman who stays because she's chosen, and chooses me back. I want a woman who loves me with her heart and soul, as I do her."

Isla's laugh is soft and broken. "You finally sound like someone worth risking myself for."

He smiles, relief and affection threading together. "I was hoping you'd say that."

She doesn't answer with words.

She reaches for him instead, fingers curling into the front of his shirt, anchoring herself to something real. He exhales against her hair, arms wrapping around her like he's been holding himself apart for far too long.

This time, she doesn't feel like she's disappearing.

She feels seen.

They pull back just enough to look at each other, foreheads touching.

"What happens now?" Isla asks.

Callum's smile is gentle. "Now we figure it out together."

She nods, emotion swelling in her chest. "No managers. No castles making decisions for us."

"No," he agrees. "Just us trusting one another. Choosing each other always. I love you, Isla, and can't live without you."

Isla closes her eyes, breathing him in. "I choose you, Callum. I love you, heart and soul."

For the first time in her life, love hasn't asked her to compromise herself.

"Please don't ever leave me again like that," Callum says softly against her hair.

"I won't," she promises. "We'll find a way together."

"Yes," he says as his lips cover hers and she surrenders to him, knowing that she's found a lasting love. One that won't disappear.

For the first time in her life, love hasn't asked her to compromise herself.

It's asked her to trust.

And this time, she does.

CHAPTER 28

They stand together beneath the lights, the hush of the audience settling into something expectant and reverent.

Isla sits at the piano, her fingers hovering for a heartbeat before she lets them fall. The first notes unfurl, clean, deliberate, alive, and then Callum joins her, his guitar threading through the melody like a promise kept. They don't look at each other right away. They don't need to. The music knows where it's going.

This is not inheritance.

This is choice. The music began with her father, but in her hands and Callum's, it becomes something shared, love shaped gently from what he left behind, a quiet reverence for the man she never truly knew.

The audience listens as if holding its breath. The piece builds, swells, resolves, not into triumph, but into belonging. When the final note fades, the silence lasts a beat longer than applause ever does. Then the room erupts.

Backstage, Isla laughs, breathless and bright, and Callum catches her around the waist, lifting her just enough to make her yelp. They're giddy in that way that comes from doing something hard together and surviving it intact.

"We did it," she says, as if she still needs to convince herself.

"We keep doing it," he replies. "That's the trick. We love music, we love each other, and we show the world what we can do together."

"I love you, Callum," she says almost reverently.

"I love you more. Now let's go home," he says.

"Home?" she asks.

He doesn't hesitate. "Home."

The drive is familiar now, the road curving toward stone and sky. The castle rises out of the dusk, solid and welcoming, not a monument, not a test, but a place they return to because they want to. Because someone is there.

Inside, the air is warm. Lived-in. Music stands lean against walls. A kettle hums. There are signs of presence everywhere, shoes by the door, a scarf on a chair, a guitar resting where it can be reached.

Six months ago, they were married on the lawn of the castle. Her mother even came from the States. It was a simple ceremony with friends, music industry guests, and old friends of her father.

Now when they're not touring, they reside here in the castle, but it's been changed. Updated to reflect their lives and not Keir's. It's now a place that feels like home.

Isla pauses, taking in their sanctuary. "It doesn't feel like it used to."

Callum squeezes her hand. "Good."

"It feels good. Like the walls are accepting."

"It's our home," he says quietly. "Yours and mine."

They set their cases down and move through the rooms together, not as caretakers of a legacy, but as two people who showed up and stayed. The castle holds them, yes, but gently, without demand.

Love, Isla has learned, isn't inherited. It isn't claimed by stone or paper or name.

It's chosen.

And tonight, like every night, they choose each other.

Going into their bedroom, she sighs and looks around the room they had decorated together. There are painted musical notes above their bed. Their song of love to one another.

A smile fills her face as Callum walks in. "Are you happy?"

"Oh, yes, my love," she says, moving into his arms. "I love our life together, making music together. I even love this old castle now."

Callum kisses her. "We've made it our home. Even the castle feels happier now. I only wish your father had been here to see our happiness."

"Me too," she says. "But in some ways, I think he brought us together. He knew that you would help me see him as the man he was and help me heal from the pain of his absence."

Callum puts his forehead to hers. "Love, I think you're right. I've never considered it that way before, but your father did bring us together. And I'm so thankful he did."

"I think it's time you took me to bed," she said softly.

"All I want to do is make you happy," he said, kissing her softly.

After all the turmoil, Isla knows that she and Callum have made the castle theirs in every way, and soon, she hopes they will have a little one running around listening to the music that reverberates within these walls. And their child will know both of their parents.

* * *

THANKS FOR READING INHERITING a Scottish Castle. I so wanted this book to be funny, but these characters just wouldn't let it be.

I loved the musical aspects of their relationship. I hope you enjoyed the book. Authors love it when you leave a review, whether you liked the book or hated it. Next up is **Inheriting an Alaskan Gold Mine** in late 2026.

231

INHERITING AN IRISH GROOM

Sometimes you wonder if the great Oz enjoys totally disrupting life.

When Aisling O'Byrne got the call, she'd been on her way to her last presentation at a small bookstore in Hollywood, running on caffeine, ambition, and the sheer force of dreams that just wouldn't quit.

Patrick Wright—the Patrick Wright—was finally going to meet with their firm.

After months of chasing him across time zones, trade shows, and inboxes, the bestselling thriller author and his agent were in New York, and Aisling had snagged the meeting. If they landed him, it wouldn't just change the trajectory of the small indie publishing house she worked for—it could launch *her* into the editorial career she actually wanted. No more playing salesgirl with a smile and a suitcase full of Author Reader's Copies. She could finally be the one *acquiring* books instead of just *peddling* them.

Racing to the airport, she'd called Michael and Samantha and told them to be prepared. Patrick Wright would be meeting with them this very morning. She hadn't slept on the plane. Instead, she'd spent five hours constructing the perfect pitch and three more mentally practicing how to *not* fangirl when she met him. Her feet ached from sprinting through LAX in heels. Her nerves were fried, but her heart was thundering with the kind of excitement that made her feel *alive*.

She couldn't wait to see Michael.

He hadn't answered when she'd called from the airport last night, but he'd sounded off earlier that day—distracted, maybe a little drunk—but thrilled, nonetheless. They both worked at the same company. This meeting could mean a *promotion* for him too. Their lives—the one they'd planned—could finally begin. Wedding. New apartment. A lifetime of commitment. The works.

She smiled as the cab rolled to a stop in front of his building. The New York skyline blinked overhead, busy and buzzing like always. Still, a small part of her—tucked behind the exhaustion and nerves—longed for a place that didn't run 24/7. A quieter life. One that gave her room to breathe.

One she could build with the man she loved.

She tipped the cabbie, grabbed her suitcase, and nodded to the doorman, who opened the door for her. "Good morning, James."

"Good morning, Miss O'Byrne."

As she walked through the lobby, she knew this was not the apartment building she wanted to live in. She and Michael hadn't lived together yet, but it was only a matter of time. She had a key, a drawer, a toothbrush, and dreams.

And in a few hours, they'd both be sitting in front of Patrick Wright, pitching a future that would skyrocket their careers.

She took the elevator up to his floor, heart fluttering like the inside of a new hardcover. The building smelled like fresh paint and overpriced rent. Her reflection in the mirrored doors looked a little wild but determined—red curly hair in a sleep-deprived bun, tired green eyes, lipstick applied with the precision of someone who'd done it in a cab.

This was the start of everything.

She let herself in with her spare key, already planning to shower, change, and wow the author of the decade. Today was a special kind of day, and she wanted to look her best.

But the second the door opened, her steps faltered.

The apartment was a disaster zone. Takeout containers scattered. The reek of tequila soaked the air like cheap cologne. Clothes on the floor. Women's panties. A bra. His underwear.

No. Just no.

Her stomach twisted. Michael wasn't a neat freak, but this had the makings of a liquor-soaked affair. What were women's clothes doing on the floor? Her stomach clenched, her heart beating wildly.

He must still be asleep.

She walked toward the bedroom, suitcase bumping quietly behind her, still holding on to the sliver of hope that maybe—just maybe—he'd had a rough night and just needed a coffee and a shower.

What she got instead?

Two naked bodies. One bed.

Her fiancé.

Her boss.

Aisling froze. She swallowed a sob.

Her brain tried to make sense of it—Michael, sprawled on his side, arm slung across Samantha Lee, her boss, who was snoring softly with her perfectly blow-dried hair splayed on *Aisling's pillow*.

Two empty tequila bottles.

An open box of condoms.

She blinked.

Then blinked again.

Her throat closed around a sound she didn't make. Just a sharp inhale that tasted like betrayal and bile.

Her stomach clenched, and for a moment, she feared she was going to throw up.

Her hands started to shake.

But her mind—oh, her mind snapped into crystal clarity.

She didn't scream.

She didn't cry.

She took a long, slow breath… and *pivoted*. The son of a bitch was going to pay for what he'd done. And pay dearly.

They were still passed out. Perfect.

She walked—very calmly—to the nightstand and opened the drawer.

Inside?

The handcuffs.

Michael's favorite prop. The ones where he liked to cuff her to the bed, and then she would beg him to have his way with her. Well, she was about to have her way with him, and he wasn't going to enjoy what she planned to do.

Today, *he* was going to be the one who begged.

With a level of focus she hadn't summoned since her college finals, Aisling picked up his wrist and clicked the cuff shut then wrapped the chain around the metal pole in the middle of the headboard and snapped Samantha's hand in the other cuff. She stirred and moaned something unintelligible but didn't wake.

In the drawer, a Sharpie lay next to the keys.

Well…what could she do with this?

It would be rude *not* to use the permanent marker.

With a practiced flick of the wrist, she scrawled the word *tiny* across Michael's forehead, adding a bold arrow down his nose. On his chin, in aggressive black letters: dick.

The man didn't move, but did scrunch up his nose. How much tequila had they drunk?

Samantha got *whore* and *skank*. Very minimalist. Very chic.

Then Aisling took a picture. For personal satisfaction, of course.

She stared at the diamond engagement ring on her finger—the one he'd given her in Central Park under fairy lights and fake promises. The one where he'd said he was so proud she would be his wife and promised her that they would have a great life.

She slipped it off, her heart wrenching in pain.

A slow, wicked smile crept across her face.

She grabbed her gym bag from his closet. Inside was the old lock she used for her college locker. She slipped the ring onto it. Then she lifted the sheet on the bed and smiled. She looped it through the one place she knew he'd feel it—his beloved metal cock ring. With a snap, she closed the lock.

Let him try explaining *that* to the ER doctor.

Keys? Oh, she had those.

And they were going *with* her.

She zipped her bag, grabbed her suitcase, and glanced back at the bed.

They still hadn't moved.

Unbelievable.

She rolled her eyes and laughed—actually laughed.

Then, she snapped one more photo for the company webpage, focusing on their foreheads.

Turning, she knew she had to get out of here before she did something else even more diabolical. When she opened the door, she let it slam behind her with theatrical flair. If that didn't wake them up, they were dead.

Tears rolled down her cheeks as she walked toward the elevator. Her emotions finally overwhelmed her.

Revenge was a dish best served cold, and she wasn't finished ruining their day. Their week. But she also knew she would no longer be working for the company she loved. She'd be fired within a couple of hours.

What she would do, she had no idea. But this part of her life was over.

Moments later, from down the hall, she heard Michael's scream.

"AISLING!"

She stepped into the elevator, pressed the button, and smiled as the doors closed. Wiping her eyes, she sighed.

"Good morning, sunshine," she called sweetly. "Make it a great day."

Available Everywhere!

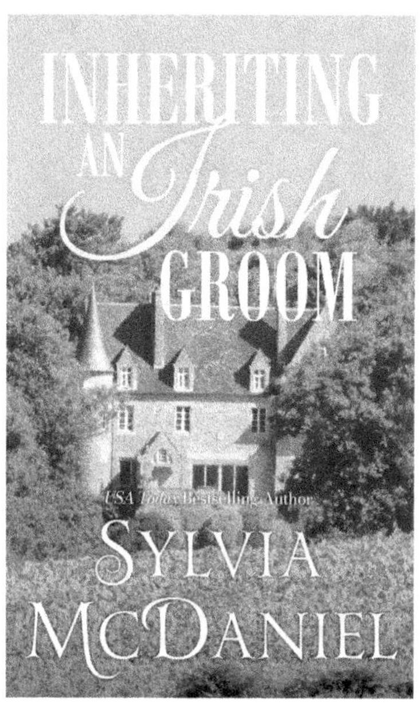

Hollywood, California

Staring at the envelope in her hand, Jennifer Moss sat in her Volvo waiting to pick up her son from the Hollywood high school baseball practice. Before she left the house, she'd grabbed the mail.

Now, an eerie sense of foreboding spiraled through her and filled her with anxiety. But then every time she received a piece of mail in which she didn't recognize the name on the envelope, her stomach churned.

Could this be from her? How many times had she gotten her hopes up for them only to be dashed? Would this be the same?

A soft breeze blew through the window on the cloudless day. For a moment, she stopped breathing as she stared at the address.

Madison Wilson, Austin, Texas.

Who did she know in Austin? Who was Madison Wilson? Anytime she received an envelope like this, her heart would pound in her chest and she would wonder if she'd been discovered.

Part of her wanted to be found, but then she would think of her life now. No one knew. It had been her secret for twenty-six years.

The memory of the house on Mustang Island overwhelmed her. She'd never returned after that summer, and since her parents' deaths, the house sat vacant. As much as she loved that place, she'd never go back because she would have to face the past.

A past that was heart wrenching and left her scared and hating her family.

Shouts from the field alerted her that the team would be leaving practice shortly. The coach always ended their practice with a pep rally. The kids were a good team and might make it to state this year. For her son's sake, she hoped so.

With a sigh, she tore open the envelope and pulled out the letter.

My name is Madison Wilson. According to the genealogy report, your DNA and my DNA are linked. It says you're my birth mother. I would like to speak to you and find out why you gave me up for adoption. I would also like to learn my medical background and even see if we have anything in common. If you are willing to speak to me, please contact me at...

A cry escaped her and the memories flooded her of that terrible day. Her name was Madison. Her heart leaped with a joy only a mother could feel.

Madison gave her address, her phone number, and even her email address.

It had taken twenty-five years, but her secret was about to be revealed. With a sigh, she stared out at the baseball field and let the memories of that day overwhelm her. How she had clung desperately to her child until her mother ripped the infant from her arms and gave her to the nurse.

She'd never seen the baby again after that day. Tears filled her eyes and trickled down her face. How many times had she thought of finding her and telling her how much she wanted to keep her? In the end, she thought it better not to disrupt her life and had done her best to move on. Now that child was grown up and wondering why she had not been wanted.

But the opposite was true.

Oh, God, how she'd wanted to keep her. To love her and raise her as her own.

That time in her life had been the worst, and she'd never forgiven her mother for forcing her to give up her child for all the right reasons. They were not what Jennifer wanted to hear.

Sometimes doing the right thing was not the easiest. And having that child taken from her arms was gut-wrenching.

Her handsome son walked across the school yard, his head down. Quickly she wiped the tears from her eyes and shoved the letter into her purse.

How was her family going to react to this news?

Her husband Ryan didn't know about her unwed pregnancy and subsequent birth. Her two smart, intelligent, beautiful children had no idea they had a half-sister. This secret had remained hidden for twenty-five years, but no more.

The door opened and her son slid in.

"Hi, Mom," he said and she could see he was upset.

"Bad day?" she asked.

"Kind of," he replied as he looked out the window of the car.

Something had been eating at him and she didn't know what. He refused to talk to her about it, and only said, *I'm okay.* But he wasn't. His grades had gone from honor roll to barely passing and she feared he was going to lose his scholarship to his favorite school.

No matter how she tried to approach him, the walls came slamming down. And today's mail wouldn't make the situation any easier. Yet, she had waited so long for this letter. So long to hear from the baby she loved instantly.

He looked at her and studied her for a moment. "Are you all right?"

"Sure," she said, wondering how he could tell something was up. "Got something in my eye a moment ago."

"Oh," he said and gazed back out the window as she pulled out of the school parking lot.

"Is Dad going to be home tonight?"

"I don't know," she said. "This morning he left early because it's his surgery day."

Alex made a noise she couldn't quite interpret.

Her husband was a leading plastic surgeon in the Hollywood community and had worked on many stars in his practice. The money he brought in had made it easy for her to stay home and raise their two children.

But the hours he worked were sometimes long, and he often came home exhausted. Lately, he seemed to work longer and longer, though he'd promised her he was going to cut back his hours.

In the twenty years they'd been married, she often wondered if she'd traded love for money. Their marriage was good, but they spent so little time together, with him working so many hours. Sometimes it felt like they were two individual people living in the same house.

And there were days she felt lonely. If not for the kids, she would spend her evenings alone. And even they were growing up and moving on with their lives. Taylor would soon finish her second year of college, and next fall, Alex would be going to a university.

"How's the team doing?"

"If we continue to win, we should make the high school play-offs," he said, staring out the window.

Alex was normally so happy and excited and eager to talk, but in the last two months, he'd withdrawn into himself and she couldn't find a way to bring him out. The kid should be so excited about his team making the playoffs, and yet he didn't act like he cared.

Something was eating at her son and she missed the happy-go-lucky young man who was eager to begin his life.

"That's great news," she said. "When's your next game? Maybe me and your dad can both attend."

Ryan had only made it to one game. One, and soon their son's season and high school career would be at an end. Sometimes she hated Ryan's job, even though their life was luxurious because of his career.

That didn't excite Alex and she knew she had to learn what troubled him.

Sometimes she wished Ryan was an accountant or even a salesman and not a busy doctor.

Maybe after Alex graduated, she would get them reservations at Cozumel and take the kids down to the beach. She doubted that Ryan would take the time off. But it would be good to spend some time with her children.

The thought of Madison crossed her mind and she wondered if she would like to go with them.

"That would be nice," he said. "The next game is Saturday morning."

That was Ryan's tee time. Surely he could give up golfing one Saturday for his son. But nothing came between Ryan and his golf.

They pulled into the drive and the gate opened automatically. She pulled into the back garage. The pool man had been here today, and maybe later tonight, she'd get in the water and swim a few laps.

Closing the garage door, they both exited the car and walked into the house, entering through the laundry room.

"Good afternoon, Mrs. Moss, Alex," the maid said to her. "Dinner is in the oven. I'm leaving for the day."

"Thank you, Esmeralda," she said softly.

Alex walked past the woman and that was so unusual for him. Normally he would hug Esmeralda and tell her the cooking was divine. But not today.

Glancing at her son, Jennifer was worried. Maybe it was time to suggest counseling. Anything to keep his grades from falling even further. Anything to keep him from losing his scholarship. Anything to bring the boy she loved back to her.

"Good night," Esmeralda called as she exited the back door.

Jennifer walked into the massive kitchen and there was a salad sitting out and a casserole ready to turn on in the oven.

"Mom," Alex said, walking back into the kitchen. "Coach said I had to give you this."

She glanced at the envelope he held in his hand.

Taking it, she opened it to the letter inside.

"Damn it, Alex," she said as she read the letter. "What is going on?"

He shrugged. "Don't know."

"If you don't bring your grades up you're going to lose your scholarship. You're about to be kicked off the baseball team. This is not my son. Tell me what's wrong."

With a grimace, he turned and walked out of the kitchen. "Maybe I want to do high school over again. Maybe I'm a loser."

"Alex, don't walk away. Let's sit down and talk about this."

He ignored her and went up the stairs to his room.

Shaking her head, she couldn't wait for Ryan to get home. They had to have a serious talk with Alex, and she had to tell him she had another child. Madison.

Reaching inside the refrigerator, she pulled out a full bottle of wine and poured herself a glass.

It was going to be a hell of a night.

Available Everywhere

Contemporary Romance
Burnett Brides Contemporary Times
Travis
Tanner
Tucker
Joshua
Jacob
Justin
Cameron
Caleb
Cody
Desiree
Burnett Brides Contemporary Box Set Books 5-7
Burnett Brides Contemporary Box Set 8-10
Burnett Brides Contemporary Box Set 11-14

Return to Cupid, Texas
Cupid Stupid
Cupid Scores
Cupid's Dance
Cupid Help Me!
Cupid Cures
**Cupid's Heart
Cupid Santa
**Cupid Second Chance
Cupid Charmer
Cupid Crazy
Cupid's Bachelorette
Cupid Games
Return to Cupid Box Set Books 1-3
Cupid Help Me Box Set Books 4-6
Return to Cupid Box Set Books 7-9
Return to Cupid Box Set Books 10-12

**The Unlucky Bride

Contemporary Romance
My Sister's Boyfriend
The Wanted Bride
The Reluctant Santa
The Relationship Coach
Secrets, Lies, & Online Dating

Bride, Texas Multi-Author Series
**The Unlucky Bride

Coming Home for Christmas
I'll Be Home for Christmas
White Christmas
Santa's Baby
All I Want For Christmas
Box Set

Inheriting An Irish Groom
Inheriting a Scottish Castle

Kissing Oaks Billionaire Brothers
The Cowboy Billionaire's Lucky Break
The Cowboy Billionaire's Fate
The Cowboy Billionaire's Playbook
The Cowboy Billionaire's Secret
The Cowboy Billionaire's Deception
The Cowboy Billionaire's Match
Kissing Oaks Billionaire Brothers Box Set 1-3
Kissing Oaks Billionaire Brothers Box Set 4-6

Lipstick and Lead 2.0
Nailing the Hit Man

Nailing the Billionaire
Nailing the Single Dad
Box Set

Secrets of Mustang Island
Secrets of a Summer Place
Secrets of a Runaway Bride
Secrets From the Past
Secrets of a Reckless Life
Secrets of a Hidden Life
Secrets of a Midnight Letter

Secrets of Mustang Island Novellas
The Summer I Loved You
When We Meet Again
Christmas at Mustang Island

The Langley Legacy
Collin's Challenge

Short Sexy Reads
Racy Reunions Series
Paying For the Past
My Christmas Soldier
Cupid's Revenge

Western Historicals
A Hero's Heart
Second Chance Cowboy
Ethan

American Brides
**Katie: Bride of Virginia

Mail Order Bride Tales
**A Brother's Betrayal
**Pearl
**Ace's Bride

Scandalous Suffragettes of the West
**Abigail
Bella
Mistletoe Scandal

Southern Historical Romance
A Scarlet Bride

The Cuvier Women
Wronged
Betrayed
Beguiled
Boxed Set

The Debutante's of Durango
The Debutante's Scandal
The Debutante's Gamble
The Debutante's Revenge
The Debutante's Santa
Box Set

**** Denotes a sweet book.**

Want to learn about my new releases before anyone else? Sign up for my New Book Alert and receive a complimentary book.

Sylvia McDaniel is a USA Today Bestselling author with over one hundred western historical and contemporary romance novels under her belt. Known for creating memorable bad boys and good girls who can't help getting into trouble, she spends her days weaving compelling tales filled with heart, humor, and unexpected plot twists. Her family-oriented stories have earned her a loyal fanbase, and she's always dreaming up new ways to keep her readers turning the page.

Married to her best friend for over thirty years, Sylvia lives in Colorado, where she enjoys hiking and taking in the natural beauty of the forest that borders their home. Their spoiled dachshund, Zeus (who has his own column in her newsletter), and brat dog Bailey keeps them company on their adventures.

Sylvia keeps close ties to her southern roots, especially when it comes to football. A dedicated fan of both the Denver Broncos and the Dallas Cowboys, she's happiest when they're winning.

Love books? Love deals? Love a little mischief? Sign up for my
Substack—it's free!
https://sylviamcdanielauthor.substack.com/
The End

9 781965 882788